Speaking *from Spirit*

D0877961

Speaking from Spirit

*Inspiring Stories and Messages from
Those Who Have Passed On*

RoseMarie Rubinetti Cappiello

BRYCE CULLEN PUBLISHING

**BRYCE
CULLEN**
PUBLISHING

PO Box 731
Alpine, NJ 07620
brycecullen.com

ISBN 978-1-935752-52-3

Library of Congress Control Number: 2014951613

10 9 8 7 6 5 4 3 2

For Cre

CONTENTS

Preface   *ix*
Introduction   *xi*

Section One: Stories of Hope and Inspiration   *1*
1: Soul Power—A Story About Dr. Mark Raphael Huber   *3*
2: Susan and Olivia—Olivia Sends Us a New Family   *8*
3: Anna Vincenza—A Simple Life   *15*
4: Lenny—A Life Worth Living   *27*
5: Nancy—Every Soul Has a Destiny   *34*

Section Two: Stories of Love, Healing, and Forgiveness   *43*
6: Larry—An Opening for Compassion   *45*
7: Baby Emily—The Opportunity   *52*
8: Thomas—Visits from the Other Side   *56*
9: Joself—The Power of Love to Heal and Transform   *61*
10: Ernie—It's Never Too Late to Say I Am Sorry   *68*
11: Blanche—Sometimes It Takes a Lifetime   *73*

Section Three: Stories of Lessons in Death   *83*
12: Rebecca's Story   *85*
13: Mandy—Finding Purpose Through Death   *91*
14: Connie—A Message of Love for My Children   *96*
15: Lisa Ann—The Power of Acceptance   *102*
16: Mary—A Healing Place for Transforming Consciousness   *108*
17: Alice—A Description of the Dying Process   *113*
18: Lucretia's Story   *119*

Section Four: Stories of the Dark Mind *131*

19: Jason—Transcending Addiction—A Return to Self *133*

20: Izzie—Finding Compassion and Love
for Those Who Are Lost *140*

21: Rodrigo—Making Restitution *146*

22: Edgar—Breaking Spells *153*

Section Five: Stories for Better Living *159*

23: Anna—Shifting Consciousness One Mind at a Time *161*

24: Earth Speaks—Clarity *166*

25: A Channeled Story—Spirit Speaks to Us *172*

Conclusion *176*

Acknowledgments *179*

About the Author *183*

PREFACE

Some things that need to be said....

Some may think this is a work of fiction. In fact, it is classified as fiction—maybe? It depends on the reader. The insights and information given in each story are certainly not fictitious. However these stories arrived, and whatever your belief system may be, I encourage you to take the gifts these stories bring in whatever way works for you. In the end it doesn't really matter if this is fiction or not.

This is not a book on mediumship, psychic ability, or new age information, yet all of this is included in this book, as these were the skills and tools I used to bring this book into creation. Again, it is not my desire to change anybody's belief system or to introduce these processes, although I felt I needed to share how these stories were told to me and how I understood what I was experiencing through the course of writing this book.

None of the information in this book has been validated. There are reasons for this. I feel I wrote these stories for these spirits and that their goal is to get a message to their loved ones. The fact that they included information that is beneficial for the rest of us is just the efficiency and perfection of divinity. I know these souls will work behind the scenes to ensure that this book reaches the hands of those they want most to read it. I do ask that if anyone reading this recognizes the souls speaking in these stories, please contact me. I would love to hear more about these lovely people. The confirmation would be most welcome.

Lastly, I struggled with the introduction. I felt it was important to explain how I developed this particular set of skills and abilities—that it somehow set the foundation for this book. My fear was someone might get turned off reading about this story and not go on to the magnificent stories. This book is not about me, and I certainly don't want to cast a shadow on the brilliance of these stories. So with that said, this book does not have to be read in any order. I encourage you to pick it up and start on whatever story you feel compelled to read. Reading just one will awaken your desire to read more....

—Ro

INTRODUCTION

Over the years, many people have asked me how I became a medium or if it was always there—a natural ability. I believe that mediumship was always part of my "soul plan," but it was a latent gift that did not emerge until I was physically, mentally, emotionally, and spiritually ready to handle its power. As a child I was perceptive, and my intuition and psychic ability often spoke to me through my dreams. This often happens when people have undeveloped, unclaimed, or untrained psychic abilities, but like most people, I viewed these occurrences as random and completely beyond my control. I did have some very powerful and insightful visionary dreams as a kid—I still do—but I have since learned to channel my psychic, intuitive, and mediumistic abilities beyond my dream state.

In February 1995, when I was thirty-three years old, I was in a minor car accident that would completely redirect my whole life and eventually lead me to discover an innate ability to speak to and hear spirit. On that cold morning, I had no idea of the mystical journey that was about to unfold for me, or that my soul was choosing to embark on this very magical path.

Background

I grew up in a New Jersey suburb five minutes outside of New York City—a town called Lyndhurst. To this day, I live there with my family. It is a small, middle-class, blue-collar town where everyone knows everyone. My husband and I have lots of ties and roots to our town and community, and I am more known as Miss Rose, the dance teacher, than I am as a psychic medium. I come from first generation Italian American Roman Catholic parents. My father, Roger, who I adored, was a World War II vet from the greatest generation. He was a hardworking family man and proud father of four beautiful daughters—me being the third of the bunch. My mom, RoseMarie (who I am named after), was a waitress in the best restaurant in Lyndhurst. She worked long before most mothers did and loved her work like a vocation or calling. My dad worked various jobs, never really making anything a career, but both had an impeccable work ethic that my sisters and I inherited.

My sister Lucretia was twelve years older than me, Donna nine years older, and Suzanne just fifteen months younger. Lucretia was named after my paternal grandmother; Donna after *the* Madonna herself, my mother's patron saint; and Suzanne, well, the nurse named her because my parents hadn't counted on another child, let alone another girl. My mother would often say that she got pregnant with me because she wanted a boy. She made it clear that it took her a while to get over that disappointment, even though I tried to make that up to her by being the tomboy of the house. I later gave her her first grandson, Nicolas, and she claimed him as her own. He was the sun and moon to her, and they often relished ganging up on me. Still, I love the bond they shared and think of their connection with fond memories.

I came into a very loving family filled with an even more loving extended family. From this early life experience, I feel I have recreated, attracted, and experienced loving environments and people over and over again my whole life. My aunts and uncles adored and doted on me. My cousins, who were much older, treated me as a living doll. They nurtured, loved, guided, and cared for me. Their children, who are slightly younger than me, were and still are my comrades, besties, teammates, and journeymen.

My sisters and I are very close. Italian girls don't really know how to separate from family. We stay close, enmeshed even—sometimes in a good way, sometimes not! I had a great upbringing and early life. I enjoyed school, had lots of friends, was popular and outgoing in high school, and had a very fun young adult life. I was a regular patron of the disco scene and spent summers at the Jersey Shore. My friends and I could have been the original *Jersey Shore* cast! I even traveled with a dance company to Europe and Japan.

I always felt older than my years. In fact, I didn't feel my "right" age until I turned forty. Some people never grow up, but I felt I was born grown up and had to wait until I physically caught up. I think people sensed this too. I was always with kids older than me, and most adults could relate to me very well. Lots of people would confide their troubles to me, even my teachers. Whatever I said and wherever it came from, seemed to help them feel better. And sometimes, their life would even get better after our "talks." If I sensed spirits, I wasn't aware of it consciously. I did always feel very close to *my God*, and I always felt safe, secure, and protected. I say *my God* because I believe everyone has their own image, perception, and interpretation of divinity, and hopefully their own personal and intimate connection with said divinity. I am aware that I was never afraid of death or dying—not my own, not my loved ones. I never knew where that came from until I became mediumistic. My first personal experience with death was when I was fifteen and my beloved Aunt Grace died. I was sad, and of course I did not want her to go, but I understood this was a part of life and that she was okay. I never questioned what would happen to her; I just knew she was beyond her suffering and was fine. I was aware that I did not think like most people, that I perceived this world from a very different angle, and that I could understand stuff most people couldn't. Most people found this very refreshing and re-assuring. It was not like I was telling anyone how to think, but I could explain things beyond a literal sense, and it was somehow comforting and uplifting for them.

In 1988, at twenty-six years old, I married Nick's dad, Joe, and settled into adult life. We had Justine in February 1991. Her entrance into this world came with a crisis, and it was the first time I ever con-nected consciously to my intuition. The day she was born I was mak-ing a turkey breast to bring to my sister Suzanne, who had just given birth to my niece Alyssa. My plan (hear God laughing) was to go for my weekly doctor's appointment, then drop the turkey breast to her and visit my new goddaughter. I was three weeks away from delivery, and when I was leaving the office I mentioned that the baby had been quiet and had not moved much since the night before. The next thing you know, I was being whisked back into the examining room and strapped to a fetal monitor. Her heartbeat was strong and clear, but she was limp and not moving. Before I knew it, I was at Mountain-side Hospital being induced, and that night at 11:04 p.m., Justine Marie Rubinetti Sebastiano was born. There was merconium in the amniotic fluid, and they attributed her lack of movement in utero to this. No one could explain why she had merconium. This usually hap-pens when a baby is overdue, and here I was almost three weeks early. Something didn't feel right, but I was told she was fine and that I was just being a nervous mother. I was very emotional, weepy, and a little irritable (my now ex-husband may say I was more than "a little"). I attributed this to the stressful, rushed, and emergent experience of her birth. Still, I called my pediatrician as soon as we got home and made an appointment. He was a very wise older gentleman who was more than just a trained physician; he was a healer of the highest order. Upon his examination of her, he sent us immediately to Hackensack Hospital, and Justine was admitted into the neonatal unit. He didn't create a panic, but he let me know in no uncertain terms that something was very wrong. As soon as we were admitted, testing began. No one was clear what was wrong; they just knew it was something very serious. We spent the better part of that week having test after test. They were not sure if she had something called a hemangioma or if she had an internal hemorrhage or had absorbed an undeveloped twin. I was beside myself and could not believe this was happening. In the middle of all this, a friend of my sister's called me. I am still not sure how this came about, but our conversation was an epiphany for me. She kept asking me to tell her what my intuition was telling me. I was crying and was so confused and frightened. I just kept saying, "I don't know. I don't know." She relentlessly kept asking, "What does your mother instinct say?" Finally, I said, "That there is something serious, but she is going to be all right. She is going to survive." At that point, Mary said, "I will believe that for you until you can believe that for yourself," and with that I have never spoken to her again. It was the first time I had ever consciously tapped into my intuitive center. Two days later, after an angiogram of her liver, the doctors informed us that Justine had a tumor in her liver, which they believed was a form of fetal cancer. We were told she may not survive surgery, but she would surely die without it. If she did survive the surgery, the prediction was a year of chemotherapy and radiation—ON A NEWBORN! WTF! My first thought was, "How could I have been so wrong? I couldn't have been more wrong if I tried."

Surgery was scheduled for March 2, my twenty-ninth birthday. On the morning of the surgery, as Joe and I sat in the waiting room, I seethed with anger at my God. *How could you do this? Soul Train* blared on the TV screen, and I was furious and agitated—with *Him* and myself for believing my false intuition. I noticed a *People* magazine on a table, and something about it caught my eye. On the cover was a story about Elizabeth Glaser, who had contracted AIDS through a blood transfusion and then unknowingly passed it to her daughter through breastfeeding and to her son in utero. Reading the story moved me deeply and humbled me immediately. My heart began to open and soften again, and I snapped out of my rage and regained my perspective. "Okay, God, thank you for showing me this story. I will stop feeling sorry for myself now. You win. Your will be done." Well, I might have added a few curse words in there too, but they might have been too inappropriate to write. I notice, whenever I get too lost in my fears or ego despair, something comes along to pull me up and out of my negative emotions or thinking. I call it a spirit life line. Since that time, I have often received and witnessed others getting a spirit life line too. It is sort of an intervention.

Soon after this, the nurse came to the waiting room. It had been three and a half hours. They told us the operation would last at least five hours. I did not take this as a good sign and once again began to slip into despair. Joe and I both crumbled and braced ourselves for the worst, but as I looked out the window, the sun began to shine and the sky all of a sudden became very clear. We had been having a raging storm—torrential rain and wind—and then all of a sudden it was as if the clouds parted and everything turned beautiful. In that instant I knew everything was going to be all right. The doctor appeared right after this and informed us, "It was just a tumor in the right side of her liver. We removed the whole right lobe, so she has half a liver, but it will grow back. She did not need to be ventilated or to have any transfusions, and, oh, it was not cancerous." I grabbed this man by the scrubs and screamed, "What did you just say?" Five minutes later, we were doing cartwheels in the hallway. Two weeks later I took that baby home, and she was a normal newborn in every way. She was born six pounds nine ounces, and at one month old she was just five pounds four ounces. That tumor had been a full pound. I had promised the surgeon that if she survived, I would have her write him a thank you note on her eighteenth birthday—and she did. She has now grown into a beautiful young woman and has never had an ounce of trouble with her liver since. It was truly a miracle, and I have never doubted my intuition since.

I went about planning my life pretty much like everyone else, deciding my career path from my mind and working towards that goal. Little did I know that my soul was working behind the scenes through my unconscious to bring my destiny or soul plan into play.

My career path started with a desire to become a professional dancer. I was going to shake off my little town and travel the world—a very *It's a Wonderful Life* sort of dream. When I was nineteen years old, I traveled with the Tommy Finnan Dance Company to Portugal and Japan, but I was soon disillusioned with life on the road. When I returned home, I unknowingly began a career in the fitness industry. It was, after all, the early eighties, and health clubs and leotards were all the rage. I got jobs teaching aerobic dance in various health clubs in New York City and Northern New Jersey. Soon I felt compelled to return to college and get my degree in physical education. I play no sports and am the most nonathletic person you could imagine. It made no sense to my parents. Hell, it really made no sense to me, but they supported my decision. I switched majors and got my degree in phys ed from Montclair State University. Looking back, I realize a lot of my life was guided through that compelling feeling, and I now know that it was my soul speaking to me and guiding me, even when I was completely unconscious to it. Everything I experienced was (and still is) a stepping stone for the next piece. There were no mistakes and no bad choices; every experience was necessary and led me forward. I made a nice living in the fitness field and thoroughly enjoyed what I did. It was a career, and I thought I was settled and moving forward—that is until that car accident changed my course.

At the time of the accident, I was a single mom to Nick and Juss, and the severe whiplash impeded my ability to work in fitness. Not working was not an option. My strong and fit body was now, for the first time in my life, physically limited, and I needed to find a way to work around that. I was forced to focus on exercises that my body could handle and that I could use in my fitness career. I started to take yoga classes to help my injured body. My body seemed to like this form of exercise and even seemed to know it innately. Maybe I had been a swami in another life? My first brush with yoga had come through my father years before. An avid yogi and fitness enthusiast, not to mention a very progressive thinker, he had introduced me to yoga and meditation in the late eighties. So when I returned to MSU in 1990 as a graduate assistant in phys ed, I taught yoga in the phys ed department as part of my duties. It was now resurfacing with a greater purpose. At this time in the fitness industry, yoga was not the big deal it is now, but all of a sudden it seemed like a great idea for me to pursue this path. I'm not sure whose great idea, but I listened. The fitness field did not consider yoga a serious path to physical fitness. It was considered a spiritual pursuit, and the physical component was more yin based and less yang in true yoga terms. At that time, it appeared as if there were few work opportunities for me to teach yoga in New Jersey. Still, I began to explore work options where I could instruct yoga classes instead of the aerobic or weight training and conditioning classes that I was so used to teaching. Soon the word got out that I taught yoga, and many health clubs, corporate fitness centers, and even people who just wanted a private lesson were seeking my services. It was like spirit wrote my name on some cosmic bathroom wall and work opportunities began pouring in. At one point, I felt like the only yoga instructor this side of Manhattan. I felt compelled (again) to study yoga in depth. My fitness career began to shift, and through the study of yoga, I was introduced to many practices that included energy work, shamanism, dream work and interpretation, different healing modalities, and chakras. This would later be the foundation for my mediumhsip, but at this point, I still did not know that mediumship existed. All I knew was that I was not exactly sure what I was doing, and I certainly had no idea where this was all leading or if I even wanted to go where it was leading.

That same year in late 1995, a few friends and I decided to go to a past-life regression at a yoga studio in Montclair, New Jersey. I had no expectations or prior interest in this sort of thing. Sure, we got our tea leaves read every once in a while, but this was beyond my understanding or experience. We went for kicks, but my spirit had a different agenda. I always say a door opened inside my head that night that I have not been able to close since! I had a very profound sentient and visual experience, and when I came out of it, the pain in my neck, which had been so severe for the prior nine months, was completely gone. I thought, *How miraculous*, and was so grateful, but never did I anticipate that this would lead me in any way to a life as a past life regressionist or medium. In fact, if you had said this to me at that time, I would have thought you were crazy. Thinking back, 1995 was a big year for me: car accident; career change; miraculous healing through a past life memory; oh, and meeting John—the man who would become my forever husband—in October of that year.

After that night, and without my conscious awareness or me seeking these things, spirit began to orchestrate and synchronize a spiritual lesson plan for me. It seemed the right teachers, books, friends, and information all began to appear out of nowhere. A new world and a new reality were revealing themselves to me, and I was being invited in. I didn't know what a medium or mediumship was at that time until a friend took me to see Rosemary Altea in New York City. I was fascinated but thought, *What am I here for? Why am I witnessing this?* At that time, I did not have many people who had passed, so I was not looking for a message…yet this experience did not seem random. Now I know it wasn't. I was introduced to Caroline Myss's writings and "A Course in Miracles." Wayne Dyer, Gary Zukav, and Marianne Williamson became my gurus. I studied Kripalu yoga and took classes at the Open Center in New York City. What was happening? I didn't know or care; I just knew I was growing and healing, and most of all, REMEMBERING. I was caught in a jet stream, and it was carrying me to unknown parts of myself.

In 1997, John and I married, and my life was grounded, centered, and clear. We had two more babies: Julianne in April 1998, and Gracie, named for my beloved aunt, in January 2000. Marrying John and creating a life together would now set a foundation in my personal life that would allow latent parts of my being to emerge—parts I didn't even know existed within me. I enjoyed and found meaning as a freelance yoga instructor. My body had recovered from the accident, and I felt purposeful and fulfilled. We bought our first house. I had a newfound insight and awareness of the world. I meditated every day and felt a truly intimate connection to my God and my spirit. Things were great and I was at peace. Who could want for more? Then, when Julianne was just a few months old, I had a very profound and vivid dream in which an angel, who I now know as Archangel Gabriel, told me I was going to die in two years—that my life as I knew it was coming to an end and a new one would begin. I am an extremely lucid dreamer, so I remember being in the dream and reminding myself that I was just dreaming. As if reading or hearing my thoughts, the angel corrected me, telling me this was not just a dream but a spiritual visit. When I awoke, I was not sure if this dream was literal. Was I to physically die in two years? Now again, I don't nor have I ever had any fear of death, but I needed to know so I could plan. I had small children, so if I only had two years left, I was spending it at Disney World with them and John. I was certainly not doing any more housework. I checked in with a wise woman and intuitive medium I knew, named Jinny Johnson. She explained that the angel was informing me that my life was about to completely change—that who I was and what I was, was about to become completely different. *Oh, now what?* was all I could think. Hadn't I gone through a major life change already? What did this mean? Was I going to shave my head and join an ashram and leave my children and John behind? I didn't understand this, and frankly, I was a little unnerved. I didn't want my life to change, and I worried that somehow I would be separated from family, my husband, and my children.

Soon after that dream, in early 1999, I was compelled (yet again) to open The Yoga Center in Lyndhurst, New Jersey. You'd think I would have been used to this by now, but I fretted—a lot. I had a business before and had lost a good amount of money, so I was not so interested in going back into business. Who would want to return for a root canal if the last one you had was without Novocain, right? I remember saying, "God, are you kidding? This is a small, blue-collar town; no one does yoga here. We are making a mistake." Having tremendous ambivalence and not much faith in its success, I did it anyway—and spirit proved me wrong. I had that yoga studio for nine years. It was there that I began to step into an even bigger spirit world and meet a community that I had no idea existed prior. I would host many metaphysical teachers, healers, and practitioners at this center. There was feng shui and numerology, crystals and telepathy, channeled art and psychic development, and Reiki, to name a few. Subtly, I began to shift. My perception and intuition became stronger and clearer. These teachers were opening and introducing me to a spiritual knowledge that was latent in my mind and heart. I was being homeschooled by spirit. During this time, I became a certified hypnotherapist, ordained minister, and following my father's death, a trained volunteer and counselor with Hackensack Hospice. Yeah, spirit kept me quite busy—training me, instructing me, and initiating me, all while I was running a business and raising four children. I was okay with this and thought, *Maybe this is what that dream meant.*

In the summer of 2000, I had my first mediumistic experience. A friend of mine from high school had died of ovarian cancer at the tender age of thirty-six. As I stood paying my respects to her brother, I could hear her talking to me in my head. I felt like I was having two conversations at the same time, and I was compelled to listen to her and her brother at the same time. At first I thought I was making this up, but I was aware of my own thoughts and also of her words, which I could neither predict nor control. I left the wake and sat in my car writing down her message on the back of an old envelope. It didn't mean anything to me, but it was fluid and rational. When it stopped, I could not write anything else. I sat in my car holding this scrappy paper, and I said to my God, "God, please, do not ask me to go to this woman's house and give her family this message. If you would like this message delivered, and if it is my place to do that, then bring her family to me—preferably her sister who I would feel most comfortable with." Three days after that, Diane's sister, Patty, was walking past my home as I was pulling up from grocery shopping. They lived on the other side of town, and my first thought was, *What the hell is she doing all the way over here?* My heart was racing, but I addressed her. I asked her if she could come up to my house for a minute, and she agreed. I was so nervous, having no idea how she would react to this, if she believed in this, or even if what was written would make sense to her. I explained how I was in the funeral parlor and "heard" her sister, Diane, speaking to me. I gave her the paper with the message and waited nervously for her to read it. In one part of this message, Diane spoke of birds; Patty explained that before Diane died, she had asked Diane to send her a sign (a lesson I never forgot and have used with my own relatives when the time came)—a cardinal—to let her know she had gotten to heaven and was all right. Patty said that she and a few others were having cardinal sightings like crazy. "A cardinal did you say?" I had taken notice to a cardinal in my yard for the past few days. I kept wondering why this bird was looking at me and what it was trying to tell me. Now I knew. I was receiving a sign and hadn't even known it. Patty was grateful for the message, and I was relieved how spirit orchestrated this without making me completely uncomfortable. Still, I thought this experience was a fluke—a onetime thing—and that it would go away. It didn't. After that, it was again like spirit wrote my number on the bathroom wall—it was as if everyone in spirit learned I could hear them. I was inundated with those from spirit coming through to connect with me. It was just like in the movies—I would sense them in my house, while I was in the shower, while I was working, cooking dinner, meditating…. Nighttime was the worst. When you are winding down and getting ready for sleep, your controlling mind relaxes and you are more open. I didn't sleep much as there was so much spirit activity in my bedroom. Then, alive people began coming to me for readings—how they figured out I could do this, I still don't know. I hadn't told anyone I could do this, and to this day, when asked what I do for a living, I will say that I am a yoga instructor. It is just easier. It was just like when I first started to teach yoga and was getting work like crazy. People began calling me for readings. Not claiming my mediumship at the time did not seem to be a deterrent either. What I was doing I did out of service, as a way to ease someone's loss and pain, but only when they sought me out. My fear was that I didn't know what I was doing and that I might cause someone who was suffering more pain. I was a little freaked out about this new ability, but my willingness to help someone in need, my open heart, and that relentless compelling feeling always overruled my fears. At least I understood what was happening. If I hadn't, I would have surely thought I was losing my mind and would have gone on medication. I just didn't know how to work the controls. My original teacher, Jinny, recommended that I train with Eamonn Downey, a renowned medium and teacher of mediumship and metaphysics from the Arthur Findlay College in England. In 2003, I finally accepted that this was not a fluke and was not going away, so I buckled down and began studying mediumship with Eamonn. Eamonn made a yearly trip to New Jersey, and I was lucky enough to get into his very limited class of twenty students. Through the understanding of energy and intuitive faculties, I surmised that somehow through that whiplash, my fifth chakra had opened, unleashing my clairaudient abilities, bringing forth a latent ability to hear those who had passed and to receive psychic information telepathically. It would take me until 2009 to fully own these mediumistic abilities. In the very beginning I would even deny my mediumship—that is until someone needed my and spirit's help. Although I have worked professionally as a medium for quite a while and have done thousands of readings, there was always a thought that I could quit this or that it would somehow go away. It is not that I do not have reverence for this ability; it was always that I took very seriously the responsibility of this work and its effect, both negative and positive on others. I was not afraid of what it might do to me or how

I would be perceived; it was more the yoga aspect of ahimsa—first do no harm—that had me concerned. What if I got the message wrong or made someone sadder? Still, even when I don't trust myself, spirit seems to trust me with this very important role. They (physical people and spirit people) kept showing up. It took me a long time to come to grips with my resistance and accept completely that this was indeed a part of my purpose on earth. Just recently, I moved to another level of acceptance and peace. I not only own that I am a medium, I now welcome the opportunity to use this and serve spirit and this world. There is a level of soul confidence in my mediumship that was never there before, and because of that—because I have now embraced this gift—I can serve in a greater way. These days, I feel I work for spirit, and I trust what comes through to me completely. Taking classes; studying with exceptional mediums like Eamonn, Jinny, Brian, and Simon; and most importantly, working with other mediums—especially my beloved soul sisters: Rita Gigante, Peggy Tierney, and Gale Haas—has helped me to own and accept this part of my being and this part of my life's plan. Even when I am doing the most mundane chore like washing dishes, my life is ever mystical and miraculous, and I am aware that spirit and those in spirit are always around me. Through training I have learned to set boundaries. I've learned how to work the mediumistic energy so it does not work me. While I always feel connected and aware, I am not always "on." I've learned I can tell those in spirit, "Not now. I am busy with my own life," and they will respect that.

Fast Forward—May 2010

As I sat listening to Simon James discuss theosophy and the history of mediumship, I started to get that familiar tingle in my body. I had experienced this before and knew my life was about to change. It is the compelling feeling where I know spirit is about to download a thought and give me an assignment—an offer I can't refuse.

It was May 2010 and I was attending a five-day mediumship

training class at The Journey Within Spiritualist Church in Pompton Lakes, New Jersey, with two very renowned mediums: Simon James and Brian Robertson. Here on this fourth day came a bolt of unexpected inspiration. Dropping into my mind like a fully formed concept, I clearly knew I needed to sit and write a memoir of sorts for those who are in spirit. I had no idea what these messages would be, who they would be for, or why I would be writing them; I just knew spirit wanted me to sit and dialogue with these people, and they wanted me to write it all down.

Soon after this class my mother became ill with lymphoma and passed in July, so this project spirit had given me wouldn't begin until September 2010. At this time, I had been a medium practitioner for ten years, doing anywhere from five to ten readings a week and at least one platform mediumship demonstration a month. This was in addition to teaching ten or more weekly yoga classes, taking care of my four kids, and running a house. I could barely squeeze in one day a week for this new endeavor. Still, here I was sitting at my living room computer with a lit candle, praying and meditating for direction. I didn't know what I was doing or what to expect. I had to clear my thinking in the beginning by "writing out" the thoughts in my head. Then, all of a sudden, something would happen—that shift that lets me know I am not alone, that I am connected or that I am receiving an information/energy download, like a fax machine. My fingers would start typing away, and I would be observing what was being written as quickly as I was writing it. I would hang on every word, astonished at what was coming through and the story being told to me. I did not have any control over the story, just like the first time when Diane had spoken to me at her wake, but I always had control—or choice—of whether I would sit and write or receive these visitors. Most of the time it was like any other medium reading or session, except I did not have a sitter—someone alive receiving the information from spirit— in front of me. Just like in any medium session, I would expand my energy and connect to the power (the presence of spirit), and this would allow me to go into a state of receptivity, which is required for mediumship. Through my psychic faculties, I would become aware of a presence with me, or sometimes it would simply be a completely separate stream of thought coming through my mind. There would be a flow and rhythm to the words I was hearing. I noticed after several writing sessions the tone, rhetoric, and style changed with each story. Sometimes I was transported to the lifetime being described. Sometimes I felt like the spirit speaking to me was sitting right beside me. While in this space of scribing, I was very aware none of these thoughts coming through were my thoughts or my words. I was taking dictation. If I tried to change anything (during or after), or if I tried to intercede with the writing in any way, I couldn't.

There was nothing of my own there. I was observing and listening to what was being written as much as I was writing it. What was even more unbelievable to me was that when I was done, there were no typing errors, and no editing was needed. I am a pretty bad typist, especially when I am trying to go fast, so this does not happen in any other writing I do. On the days I would write, my house was like a spirit portal. My kids, my husband, and even my dog could feel the energy shift and the presence that had been there. Even though I had often done readings in the house, the lingering energy shift was more pronounced on the days I wrote.

So on the same day every week—Tuesday—I would sit and write. After the first story—Rebecca—I Googled "Warren County, Ohio" to see if it really existed. Finding that it did, I began to look up the year she died—1986. I was told very loud and clear not to do so by a stream of thought in my mind. Somehow, it would taint the story, me, or my process in writing. I did not look up any facts again until I received the story from Jason. He had mentioned shooting "tar." I did not understand that term, so I checked with a friend to see if that was a slang term for a street drug. She confirmed it was indeed a slang term for a very deadly form of heroin. I had actually thought he injected tar. There were often references to things, time frames, and geographical places that were beyond my frame of reference. When Ernest Hemingway made his appearance, I broke the rule and researched him. I was disheartened to learn he did not have a daughter—even though he had referenced his daughter in his story. I was tempted to change what he had written, yet when I tried I could not. It was like something out of a Harry Potter movie; the story seemed protected. I later came to understand who he was referring to and understood why he said what he did. I did not check any more facts of any story after that. I am clear it is interference for me to do so. I accept on faith that the information is true and verifiable.

After writing each story, I would feel profoundly changed. I felt peaceful, uplifted, and happy. As I digested the information given, I began to live from a new space of understanding and awareness. I felt changed to my core. The intimacy I felt with spirit, divinity, God, earth, and these fine folks was (and still is) indescribable. I felt the full scope of spirit's love for me, and life began to feel magnificent and reverent. Everything in my life felt richer, fuller, deeper, and even more mystical. I began to share these stories with others to see if the effect was similar. Everyone who read them was deeply moved. Some described the stories as incredibly thought-provoking, while others related to the experiences described. Everyone who read them begged me to send more. As I progressed each week, the writing came easier. It was like a routine was forming, and this allowed me to get out of the way faster and more efficiently. Each story seemed to get richer, deeper, and more detailed. I sensed I was making a better connection to the person telling the story, and my comfort level with the process increased. Everyone who has read them has their favorite, yet almost everyone describes being moved by each story in a different way.

These lovely people who have chosen to *speak from spirit* have shared deeply personal information with us. Some need to apologize or make amends. Some just want to share an understanding about life events that one can only understand from a spiritual perspective. Those in spirit continuously reach out to us through thoughts, dreams, signs, and symbols. Now they want to tell their stories, share their soul perspective, and speak directly to each one of us. This is their legacy.

We on earth experience separation when someone we love passes. Yet these stories provide an opportunity for healing that sense of separation as well as easing our grief and suffering. We all long to connect to our loved ones who have passed into spirit. We sit and wait in hope that some proof will emerge—some sign, some symbol, and some message that lets us know they are still with us, that they are okay, that they love us. We visit mediums in search of messages, connection, and answers. We hope that our love and communication gets through to them wherever they are. We hope and pray that they are okay. Through countless readings, I can safely conclude that those in spirit feel the same way and are constantly trying to help us understand we are not separated at all. They seek to connect through mediumship and other methods to ease our pain.

These stories and messages provide an outlet for spirit to help all of us heal our wounds and live with more joy and compassion in our own lives. We are at a place in time where, collectively, we are ready for this opportunity. I believe these stories open a space for a higher understanding of life, death, the afterlife, and the dying process. Through each uplifting story, we are led right back into the heart, where peace and love are found. These gentle souls inspire us to look at our own lives and losses very differently. I am sure you will feel compelled to go on to the next story and maybe even reread this book over and over. I am, and every time I am moved. And who knows… maybe it is your loved one speaking to us all.

I also believe divinity has a goal with this book—to reach as many people in the most effective, poignant, and efficient way possible.

We often avoid having meaningful conversations about the dying process and afterlife. Many people miss the blessings in dying mindfully and consciously, as if by avoiding this understanding we will somehow be able to avoid death. Through my hospice work I have experienced the profound beauty and sacredness of life through the dying process. It can be an absolutely mystical and sacred experience, and the opportunity to experience unimaginable grace is never more present than through the death of a loved one. I have come to learn through my mediumistic abilities and through many conversations with those in spirit that every afterlife experience is different and that we create it through our mind, the same way we create our life experiences on earth. The density of earth, the physical body, and fear have less hold and impact on our thoughts after physical death, so we think, experience, learn, love, and grow from our soul because we are returned to our soul. It is like a V8 moment when everything becomes clear and we become lighter. We are returned to our true state of being, which is pure love, joy, and compassion. When we do finally remember who we truly are, we want desperately to share this with those we love so they may transcend any darkness or despair too.

There are those who have passed that would like to have their stories told so that others may live better, but I feel that they more importantly want their loved ones to know they are here and that they are okay. My first and foremost objective as a medium has always been reconnecting those in spirit to their loved ones on earth in the hopes this would lessen pain and suffering. This book contains twenty-five conscious raising stories filled with love and hope. There are many others in spirit waiting to speak to us, and I believe there are many more books to follow. I am assured this is a life-changing book. I know it has changed mine already. I am honored to have been chosen as the scribe to these profound, intimate, and transformational stories. I hope you enjoy reading them as much as I enjoyed writing them.

Peace,

Ro

SECTION ONE

STORIES OF HOPE AND INSPIRATION

1
SOUL POWER

A Story About Dr. Mark Raphael Huber

As I sat getting ready to write, I noticed all the healing angels had entered the room. Archangel Raphael was most in attendance and communicated to me directly—no words, just an intense gaze as he handed me a ball of healing white light. Archangel Raphael is most associated with physical healing and often facilitates this with the color emerald green.

"Use this whenever you would like to heal someone physically."

"How?" was my question

"Transfer the energy directly through your hands with a touch, and be completely aware that you are doing this."

"So I would reach out and hold their hand or touch them in some way? It needs to be in the physical? Not in meditation?"

"Correct."

"Who shall I do this with?"

"We will send who we want to you, and you will see them and

reach for their hand in comfort. Just know you are infusing the energy. Be cognizant of our directive."

"I understand."

*

A man enters the living room and places himself on the couch. I sensed him come in when Raphael and I were speaking. He is an older gentleman with gray hair, dark brown soulful eyes, deep wrinkles, and a heavy mustache. His head is full of salt and pepper hair. It transforms to white as he gets noticeably thinner and more wrinkled as I watch. He died very old—lung ailment or lung cancer took his life, very old, maybe nineties. He switches to his younger years—tall, dark, handsome, no stash, thin, and of course a full head of hair. He is intense, displaying an image when he was interning or in residency, serious, not at all light. He works with the bones, he says—beginning his career as an orthopedist. Instead of fractures, spirit kept sending him cancer patients, bone cancer patients. Without intention, at the age of thirty-six, he decided to study oncology and became the premier authority on bone cancers in children. His specialty: sarcoma and orthoblastomas? He pioneered major detection and screening policies. He did not work so much with the advancement of oncology treatment but with the diagnostic end. His patients appeared to heal faster and with fewer complications than most. He had two specific cases that were considered terminal and hopeless. One was a Jonathan Marks or M name? Age twelve. He had experienced the conventional treatment. When he was sent to Dr. H, he decided—was guided to—administer the same protocol. Everyone—including the boy's parents—feared it was a waste of time. This time, the same protocol worked. He survives to this day and is in his late sixties. Why did this protocol work in the hands of Dr. H? Possibly his direct link to Archangel Raphael. While he did not acknowledge this in life, he had an understanding that something greater than himself or the medicine was creating the healing. He also knew it had great intelligence, and as long as he trusted the directive, his ability, innate wisdom, and knowledge, things seemed to work out perfectly and with ease. His middle name was Raphael, given to him by his mother, under his father's protests. His mother, Mildred, had picked this name as his first, but his father would not hear of it. A compromise was reached allowing for his second name to anoint him with the essence and embodiment of power to physically heal. He never suspected this was the well from which his destiny stemmed. Neither did his mother. They both believed—just knew—a power greater than him was the healing force that worked through him. He once tried to retire, relinquishing his purpose, and focused on playing golf. After three months his soul began to wither. His only recourse was to return to his place in this world, despite his family's protests. For this man, physical death was preferable than to be alive with no purpose. What was born from this return? A very well-funded clinic for all types of cancers and cancer research. The focus centered on the patient-administer relationship more than on the search for stronger medicines. He understood it was not the potency of the medicine but the potency of the soul power of the patient and administer that would determine physical restoration. He never held any attachment to outcome regardless of his attachment to the patient. He handpicked who worked with whom and which administer worked with which patient. This was and is a pioneer facility. It does not garner much attention as it is small, personal, and close. It is the spirit model of successful allopathic pathways of healing. This is Dr. Mark Raphael Huber's legacy. He was born in 1908 and died in 1998. He was present at that clinic until two months before his passing. He had a most beautiful death surrounded by his loving family—his wife, Constance, of fifty-four years; four daughters and nine grandchildren and eighteen great grandchildren. His obituary in the *Ohio Sunday Tribunal* was a full page—mostly testimonials of the wonderful heartfelt messages from former patients, friends, colleagues, and acquaintances. He was a man with a truly successful and well-lived life.

His message as I look at him with great admiration and a yearning to replicate this in my own life is simply: "You can. Anyone can." "Ask and you will be directed." "Use your God-given talents, gifts, skills, and abilities even when you don't understand them or what they are," "Feel your purpose in your very being, not just your work or when you are working." "Do not try and understand what is happening; just witness what is happening and know that you are a partner in it." "And most of all, don't retire!"

*

I now understood why Archangel Raphael appeared to me. Could it be that Dr. Huber knew of his connection and his power to channel healing? Was Dr. Huber aware that he worked directly with the energy of Archangel Raphael? Maybe this is why Dr. Huber had such a great success with his patients' return to physical health. It was not just his knowledge, expertise, and training as a doctor—it was the healing energy that he channeled and his very essence and presence that allowed healing to occur. This is why he felt it was so important to match the right administrators, physicians, technicians, nurses, healers, and practitioners with his patients. It was sort of blending the right mix of energies that created an alchemy for true physical healing. According to spirit, we can all be conduits for healing by consciously touching another and allowing healing energy to flow through us. What if everyone realized that? What if every doctor, nurse, paramedic, mother, father, friend, and sibling did this? We can all call upon Archangel Raphael to invoke a physical healing. It may not always be what we expect or predict, but it will always be perfect. I can feel the possibilities and potential for miracles increasing just in the knowledge and awareness of this information. Will you try it?

Dr. Huber was the second story I wrote. His detailed information allowed me to picture his life in my mind the same way one visualizes while reading a story. In fact, it seems I received this story through a third party instead of directly from Dr. Huber. Spirit was describing Dr. Huber's life legacy. Or perhaps I was downloading information from the akashic records the same way Edgar Cayce had years before. There was a compassionate detachment mixed with pride and reverence coming from whatever intelligence that was conveying the story. The energy with me was uplifting and inspirational. In fact, I felt I could accomplish anything after I wrote this story…and that lingered for days. I believe the center he created still exists and that through the publication of this story, it will receive the recognition it deserves. Many more will have access to its healing force. Dr. Huber will continue his great healing work from beyond his life on earth. I believe we are ready for this form of healing now more than ever, and I feel a deep appreciation for this man who I have now met post death.

—Ro, written October 13, 2010

2
SUSAN AND OLIVIA

Olivia Sends Us a New Family

I was much more comfortable with the process of writing these stories by the time Susan came to speak with me. There was less need for me to write out the thoughts in my mind. I just sat quietly and waited for a presence to enter my living room. I felt her and wrote from my own perceptions of her first, before she began to speak. She left after our session was complete, but her energy imprint remained. My children, my dog, my husband, and even my neighbor felt a spirit presence in the house. They expressed that they felt someone was "there." This happens often when someone from spirit "visits" us. Many people confuse this with a ghost, but it is not the same thing. It is the residual energy left by any spirit presence, and it is filled with peace, love, compassion, and joy. Of course, our fears can intercept this feeling and make us believe there is something to be afraid of. What we really fear is the unknown. Still, I realized I needed to close the space—the portal, so to speak—if the living residents of this house were to feel stable and grounded!

*

To my right sits a woman with a child on her lap. She seems to have been sitting here waiting for me to get ready—waiting for me to write. From the looks of her, this picture seems to be from the early fifties. The mom has a flip do, dark hair, eyeliner, and a reddish lipstick. Her dress is a flared A-line dress with buttons leading to a belted waist. Her shoes are not too high, nor are they low heels, and they have an open toe. Her stockings have a reinforced toe, which peeks through the shoes. The little girl is more somber. She sits on her mom's lap and appears to be eight or nine years old. She has a dress similar to her mother's, but there are flowers on her dress, and she wears a little white sweater, ankle socks, and Mary Jane shoes. Her hair is long and dark, pulled back at the top, and she has banana curls. They seem dressed for picture taking.

Mom speaks:

This is a picture taken in our living room in Michigan. Olivia was eight years old at the time. I was twenty-eight. I adored her, was so proud to be her mother. I doted on her endlessly. By her expression, you can see she didn't always appreciate that. This picture was taken on Mother's Day 1958. Mother's Day was always very special for me. I always wanted to be a mother, always wanted lots of children. That, however, was not meant to be. Olivia was an only child. Back then, there was not much help for women who had trouble getting or sustaining pregnancy. The help that was available was very expensive. One didn't discuss such things openly, not like nowadays, where anything and everything is open for discussion. So we were lucky to have her, and I cherished her and devoted my life to being her mother. When she was nine years old she developed a terrible cough. We had a very rough winter, and our home had lots of drafts. She came home from school one day with a fever and flu. It took her a while to get better—almost three weeks—but the cough lingered and lingered. Eventually, she was sick again and had to stay in bed for two more

weeks. She seemed to be getting better, and by then spring was coming around. I was so glad. I thought the fresh air would be good for
her and help her recover. By mid-April she was sick again, and this
time she was diagnosed with pneumonia. She had to be hospitalized.
She lay in a tent for ten days. We couldn't touch her or hold her, or
sometimes even stay in the room with her. I had to sit outside her
room or on the other side of the room. It was torture. I couldn't hold
or touch my baby girl, and all she could do was lie there and stare at
the ceiling. She was so thin and frail, she barely ate. They were giving her nutrients to sustain her. I was often told to go home, but I
couldn't—wouldn't. The doctors and nurses would look the other way
so I could stay there until very late at night. This went against all the
rules: visiting was only 2:00 to 4:00 p.m. and 6:00 to 8:00 p.m., but I
came early in the morning and stayed late in the evening. I always left
with a very heavy heart. I would take a cab because my husband had
to work early in the morning and needed to sleep. He came right from
work, and we would eat in the cafeteria and then visit with Olivia. He
would leave at 8:00 p.m. and I would stay. He understood that I was
doing what a mother had to. It never occurred to me that she would
die. I never went into such a thought. That is what made it so shock-
ing when we got the call at 4:30 a.m. telling us that Olivia had passed
during the night. Rick had answered the phone. He told me we had
to get dressed and go to the hospital. I didn't even think to ask why…
and he thought I understood why. Poor dear; he was in shock too. We
arrived at the hospital, and the doctor on call received us. He was not
the usual doctor. His name was Dr. Tate. He asked us if we wanted
to see her, and I said, "Of course we want to see her!" I thought we
were there because she had a breakthrough and was better—I thought
we were taking her home. The mind can be very tricky—and it can
protect us from that which is unthinkable. As we walked towards the
room, Rick began to cry, and that was when I knew. It was like the
illusion was shattered, and all at once my mind comprehended what
was happening. I looked at him and then ran wildly towards Olivia's

room. The tent was off, and she was just lying so still and quiet. She looked like she was sleeping, except that she was slightly blue. My beautiful baby girl. I threw myself on her and began to weep uncontrollably. The doctor, Rick, and a few nurses had to pry me from my child and then sedate me for hysteria.

I barely remember the funeral. I don't think I made any of the plans or arrangements either. My sister stepped in to handle things, as Rick and I were completely overcome with grief. I remember sitting in my home with so many people there, consoling us. I remember being at the cemetery and having to get back into the car and not wanting to leave Olivia there all by herself. I don't remember much else. I was numb and sedated and grief-stricken.

For years, Rick and I were like zombies on automatic pilot. We eventually went back to our lives. He returned to work in two weeks, but we were not alive. We were walking ghosts. I remember thinking for the first time, *Thank God I don't have more children, because I would not be capable of taking care of them.* I completely checked out emotionally. Rick and I were like two entities that inhabited the same space; we barely saw or connected with each other, yet functioned. People tried to help, tried to intervene, tried to console, but it was as if we were dead and could not be reached.

On my thirty-fifth birthday, Rick surprised me with a trip to Italy. In my life before Olivia had died, we often talked about one day taking a trip to Italy. All of that—those plans—seemed like a lifetime ago. I had no feelings about this at all. We went that summer for a ten-day trip. Rick had been coming out of the fog a bit and was trying desperately to reconnect to me—to bring me back from the space I was left in. It's a space that is neither earth, heaven, nor hell. It is earth but not alive. It is alive but feeling dead. It has nothing in it and everything in it—only you can't feel it, touch it, smell it, and enjoy it. It is nothing. I would like to say the trip was nice, but I don't really know. I wasn't present to most of it. Rick was very disappointed. We returned to our home, and a few weeks later, a young couple moved in two houses away. She was a beautiful girl named Ellen, and she had just had a baby. As I watched the moving van unloading the truck, something happened. I felt like someone hugged me from behind. I smelled Olivia and felt her. In the years since she had died, I had never experienced that before. It was if my whole body sensed her, and I could feel sensations I hadn't in years. For a few days I wrestled with being a good neighbor and bringing a cake over to welcome this new family. It had been quite a while since I socialized and reached out to anyone, even good friends, yet I felt completely compelled to make this offering. I brought them a chocolate cake—something Olivia and I loved to make together and would often find any excuse to do so. Ellen invited me in and welcomed the opportunity to make friends. She was new to the area and had left family behind, so she was eager to make some new connections. I was hesitant but again felt compelled to stay and talk. For the first time since Olivia, I felt comfortable and at ease. I began to feel like myself again, almost like my spirit was returning to my body—like I was coming back from the dead. We visited for almost two hours before the baby woke. She brought her down for me to meet. She generously held her baby out for me to hold—her baby girl named Olivia. I wept as I took the baby in my arms. I wept not of sadness but for love and gratitude for the first time since my Olivia's death. I did not explain all of this to Ellen that day, but I eventually did. We became very close. Rick and I became sur-rogate grandparents to Olivia Marie. I watched her when Ellen went to work seven years later. I was with Ellen when she went into labor with their son, Jacob. Rick helped Tom get a job in his company when the company he worked for laid him off. It was years after our first meeting that I told Rick about the hug I received from our Olivia on the day Ellen and Tom moved in. He did not dismiss it as I thought he would. Instead, he was touched deeply by this and cried a final cry that day. He confided to me that I was not the same wife he had had prior to them moving in. He had lost me when Olivia died and some-how he felt I was reborn when Ellen, Tom, and Olivia Marie arrived.

I was not the old Susan; I was somehow a new Susan.

Our lives had taken a new turn. I felt purpose again. We became engaged with life once more, and we were given a new opportunity to enjoy life again. We lived there until we passed, Rick in 1999 and me in 2003. We left everything we had to our lovely grandchildren—Olivia Marie and Jacob. They became our pride and joy. We were so grateful to have recipients for all the love we had in our hearts. We often tried to explain to Ellen and Tom what they had done for us, but words never captured the truth. They thought that they were the lucky ones, having us embrace them and support them in their life, but we know better. They returned life to us. I know for us, it was a divine gift—a second chance orchestrated by God.

Olivia Marie was the last face I saw before leaving this earth, and my Olivia was the first face that greeted me in heaven. My life came full circle and has been fulfilled.

—Sue

*

As I wrote this story, I could never imagine where it was going. I listened intently, hanging on to every word, wanting to know how this would turn out. It was devastating for me to hear of Olivia's death. Being a mother, this story hit close to home for me, and I could feel Susan's pain and sadness. I still cry every time I read it. Susan conveyed her feelings and experience so clearly. I went through every emotion with her. We call this sympathy, and it is vital to our human experience as it allows our hearts to open and deepen to the depths of compassion within us. I had a child that almost did not survive, so I related to her anxiety and worry while she helplessly waited in the hospital. This similar experience allowed me to connect to my sympathetic response; however, one does not have to experience something firsthand to offer compassion through the process of sympathizing. I remember feeling I would not be able to go on if my child died. But this story shows how spirit works in the most unimaginable ways, creating opportunities for healing and restoring balance. Life and new beginnings can come at any time, even after such a tragic loss. Olivia sent her parents the gift of this family, which helped them to heal their grief and open their hearts again. From spirit, Olivia compelled her mother to follow her heart and to open to the love this family could offer. If we allow spirit to help us—to guide us—we will be given opportunities to experience love and joy in the most unexpected and profound ways. This story shows we can find meaning and purpose in our lives no matter what the circumstances. It must have taken great courage and strength for Susan to do so, and in the end she found the channel for all the love and joy in her heart. She found her way back to Olivia too. I hope this story inspires and renews hope to anyone suffering through grief that life can begin again and that love and joy can return.

—Ro, written May 5, 2011

3

ANNA VINCENZA

A Simple Life

Today it took a while to get clear and to expand my energy enough to come to a place of connection. Mediums and healers often "tune in" to our own energy and get clear and centered before we open to spirit. It can take just a moment, or in my case on this day, a little while longer! It is like clearing away our own junk and distractions so we may come from our most centered place, free from our own perceptions, interpretations, worries, fears, and limits. We also learn to "sit in the power." The power refers to the power and presence of spirit. This process is where we expand our energy and connect to the omnipresence of divinity that is always around all of us. It is sometimes described as the force of unconditional love and serenity. The yogis call it a state of bliss, nirvana, or enlightenment. It is everywhere, and with practice, one can learn to connect to this force. People who pray (regardless of religious affiliation), chant, or meditate are often familiar with this power. Mystics, healers, and deeply spiritual people, to name a few, often sit in the power. It is profound and recognizable, and once you experience it, you are forever changed. It is an unforgettable and life-altering experience—one you will seek to visit over and over again.

Any medium worth anything is trained to tune in and hold the power. This allows the presence of divinity to come through and open a space for profound healing. In order for true mediumship to unfold, one must develop the ability to sustain the presence and power of spirit. It is the ability to be present in the power of spirit that allows mediums to connect with those in that dimension. Like a current, the power builds and holds the connection. It is through the awareness of this presence that mediumship occurs.

On this particular day it took a bit, but then I began to feel some-one connect to my thoughts. It started slowly, but it felt like a down-load of information coming into my consciousness from a woman. I believe she has tried to connect to me before, but because I was not in the space to write, I let the connection go. Writing this story was so different than the others. I had to stop and restart and wasn't sure if I'd be able to do that. It took me two days to get it all in. Anna was determined to share her story….

*

My name is Anna Vincenza, and I was originally from Italy. I came to this country—the United States—when I was a twelve-year-old girl. I came with my mother and younger brother. My father had come seven years earlier. I hardly remembered him. I did not want to leave my family or friends. I loved my hometown, which was really just a village right outside Naples—a village called Nuencini. I did not want to leave my school or my friends or even my goats.

We had goats in the home where we lived. But my father had sent for us, and we had to obey. I know my mother felt the same way. She did not want to leave her family, especially her mother. They were very close. My grandparents lived just next door to our small stone house. My grandfather helped to build my house when he was a young man. They gave it to my parents when they wed. My grandparents were very present in our lives. We ate dinner with them almost every night, and after my father left for America, we practically lived in their home. My father had not been back to Italy since he left. This was not uncommon at that time—for the man to leave and settle in a new place and then send for his family back home. My father worked in a restaurant in America, starting as a busboy and then making his way to waiter and then to wine steward. He was a smart man—not educated, but wise and savvy—and he was noticed and liked by people with power and influence in the US.

We landed in Ellis Island on June 12, 1909. It was hot and smelly, as I remember. There were a lot of people there. Many ships from other countries had come in that day, and we were all transported to this processing station. Everyone looked confused to me except the people that worked there—they just looked annoyed. My mother was unsure where to go and was directed here and there. At one point we were almost separated. That would have been horrible, as I may have never found her. There were people crying, and we had heard some were stuck there for days waiting for relatives to come for them. You couldn't leave without someone coming for you. There was a place where those who came to receive you waited—it looked like a holding pen. It took a long time for us to get to the line where we could be processed. We were tired, hungry, and dirty from the boat ride. The accommodations on the boat were bare minimum for survival. And our passage had been rough with lots of rain and storms. Very unpleasant, but what could I say? I was just a child—a girl at that. No one would tolerate a complaint from me. My mother was very afraid of being robbed on the ship, or worse. This was not uncommon, as there were not many people willing to stand up for you, or any real rules of behavior to follow. Even if there were, there was no one to enforce them. My mother had never been away from her parents except for her honeymoon, and that was with my father. She was a lone woman with two children, and I could sense her feelings of vulnerability and insecurity. I just hoped no one else could. She barely slept the whole trip over as she watched over us to make sure we were safe. Not that she would have been able to fight anyone off or anything. My mother was not fierce or assertive in any way, and I don't know what would have happened or what she would have done if anyone had meant us any harm.

My dad greeted us, and my mother collapsed into his arms. I remember watching them, realizing that they had loved and missed each other for seven years and what a sacrifice it was for them to have been apart. I wondered at that time what would make someone do this—take such a risk, follow the unknown, leave your family?

We went to my father's apartment in a part of New York City that would later be called Little Italy. At the time it was called Downtown, The Hook, or Fish Village. There were very tall buildings—apartments and sweatshops and some farms. I had never seen such big buildings before. It was hot, crowded, and smelly again. Lots of people, more than I had ever seen in my village, and they were all outside yelling at each other and over one another. We had to go all the way up to the eighth floor of this building. The hallway smelled of pee, and there was coal on the floor and in the corners. The door to the apartment was red, and when you put the key in you had to push on the door at the same time for it to open. We were on what would now be Varick Street off of Canal. When we were coming in, people would open their doors and look out. Some spoke to my father, some just looked, and others slammed the door closed. The window was open and there was no screen—my mother immediately told us never to go near that window. It was a small room with a kitchen and a small bedroom. The bathroom was down the hall, and all the people on the floor used it. My father had a radio, and when I saw that I thought maybe he was rich. We did not have a radio in Italy, but our house was certainly nicer than this. My mother did not seem thrilled with this place, but she was thrilled to be with my father and thrilled we were all together again. My brother had never met my father, as my mother was pregnant with him when my father left. It was clear we were all going to have to adjust to this new life and to each other.

It was hard at first, so noisy, so crowded, and you weren't supposed to speak to anyone you didn't know. For me that was everyone. I was used to my village where everyone knew each other and everyone certainly knew your mother and father. I could sense there was danger here, and this was a new feeling to me. My father worked a lot. He would leave about 10:00 a.m. every morning and not return until one or two in the morning. My mother was lonely and sad. She missed her family and my father. She was too afraid to venture out alone, and when she did go out with my brother and I she was rushed because she was afraid that she would lose one of us. We didn't go very far— maybe down or around the block because she was afraid we would get lost and not find the way back. She spoke no English, and the Italians that lived around here spoke a different dialect than we were used to. My brother and I started school in the fall. My mother did not want us to go, because she would be even lonelier. We weren't sure where the school was; we just followed the other kids to school. Getting home was trickier because we had to remember who lived on our block. After a while we got used to it and knew our way to and from school. We started to make friends and learn English—there was no speaking Italian in school, not even to each other. There was no speaking any other language at all except for English. You had to learn. I made friends with a Polish girl who lived south of Houston Street. She was pleasant and had been born in America. Her parents had lived on the East Side of Manhattan when they first came as children, then moved into the Downtown area. It was considered a step up. She helped me to learn the American ways. My brother made his own friends, but the poor kid really suffered in school. He was not very smart and had a hard time learning. The language barrier was no help to this. I started to do some of his work for him, but when he would be called on in school he had no idea what the teacher wanted from him. It became a problem. The teachers were baffled as to why his work was better from home but on tests he did so terrible. He would often be hit or punished by the teachers—that was frequent back then—for being insubordinate. They thought he was doing this on purpose. So I stopped doing his work for him, realizing it was costing him more than helping. He quit school in the sixth grade and went to work with my father in the restaurant. By this time, my father was the maître d' and made more money. We moved into a better apartment on Smith Street, Brooklyn, and my brother and I shared a bedroom, and my parents had their own room for the first time since we moved to the US. My mother had taken a job at a sewing factory. My father allowed this because she was so lonely and depressed with him working and us in school all day. He felt it was better than having her go crazy. She made some friends. There was an AnnaMaria that was from a village close to ours back in Italy. To her this was like having a sister here. They worked together. AnnaMaria's husband had been killed working in the fishery, and she had to work to support her three children. My mother often gave her pay to AnnaMaria to help her out. Not that we didn't need it, but my mother had my father to provide for us and felt she needed it more. AnnaMaria was very grateful and always let my mother and father know it.

When I was sixteen, I left school and began working in the restaurant as an assistant cook. Girls were not usually allowed in the kitchen of the restaurant, but the owner liked my father, and I showed a real affinity for dessert making. The head chef made complaints at first but soon realized not only did I really like this, but I had a talent for it as well. He began to take me under his wing and show me techniques—he was training me, and neither of us realized it. When I was twenty-two and showing no signs of interest in marriage, my parents began to worry. My mother was seventeen when she married my father, so to her I was an old maid. She blamed the fact that I was always working and didn't have time to look nice and attract a husband. My father told her he introduced young eligible men to me all the time at the restaurant but I practically ignored them, waiting impatiently to get back to what I loved, and that was creating beautiful, artistic desserts for the customers. I hardly made any money, but I wasn't there for the money; I was there because I really loved what I was doing—and I was very good at it. I was a career woman in a time when women did not have careers. No one called me that, nor did I realize that is what I was or what I wanted, but it was true. My parents eventually made me cut back my hours, and with that they began to push me towards AnnaMaria's son Carmine Jr. He was a few years younger than me but had been working as an apprentice butcher since he was fourteen years old. I wasn't in love with him, but he was pleasant, so when my parents and his mother suggested we get married, we did. When I look back on my wedding pictures, there is absolutely no expression on my face that day. I was completely emotionless—just doing what I was told. My parents got us an apartment in the building down the block. By this time, my father had saved to buy a small modest home in Bensonhurst, and I was leaving that bedroom I shared with my brother to go live with Carmine and share a bedroom with him. It was after I was married that I realized I had no attraction to men in a sexual way. I had no idea what that meant, but I knew that when my husband touched me it did absolutely nothing for me. Of course I did not express this—these things were not talked about, and even if they were, I wouldn't have known how to put it into words. Then the most devastating thing happened: my husband refused to let me go back to the restaurant to work. He felt it was an insult to his manhood that I would even want to. Watching his mother all those years work and slave made him even more resolved that no wife of his would ever work. I was miserable. When I tell you there were days that I wanted to throw myself out the window but was too afraid that I would just injure myself and not die…we were only on the second floor. I sat in all day and stared out the window. I felt like I was dying inside. My soul ached and longed to be in the restaurant. The only time I was remotely alive was on Sundays when we had dinner at my parents' house and my father and brother would go on and on about the restaurant and what was happening. My father and mother knew something was wrong. My father had seen the joy in me when I was at the restaurant, and even though he didn't understand, he intuitively knew the source of my malaise was that I was no longer there.

In 1925, a former customer of the restaurant came to my father and offered to put him up in business. He had made it big with some overseas ventures and was looking to invest. Luigi's Restaurant in Brighton opened on July 25, 1925. When I had worked in the restaurant, I had made special zablione for this man when he would come in. When he and my father made these business arrangements, I decided to make him this treat from my home. Carmine and I had bought a home in what is now the Cobble Hill section of Brooklyn, and my mother-in-law, AnnaMaria, lived with us along with our son, Donato, named after Carmine's late father. As I made the zablione, I felt the life coming back into me. Buying this home, having a good husband, even the birth of my child did not pull me back from the funk I had now grown used to living in. Here I was in my kitchen, creating this dessert—something I had completely stopped doing once I left the restaurant—and I was coming back from the dead. When I took the dessert to the new restaurant for the man to have, my father instantly saw the change in me. He looked at me and started to cry. I had never seen my father cry before, and I didn't understand it, but when he hugged me, which he also never did, I knew I was feeling something for the first time in a very long time—from him and from me. That night he stopped by my house with the excuse he wanted to see the baby. He had a glass of wine with Carmine and a steak that Carmine had brought home from the butcher store he now owned. He praised Carmine for being such a good husband, father, and son and told him no father could want better for his daughter. He thanked him for giving him such a beautiful grandson and a worry-free mind—that he would never have to worry about me or Donato's future with him. He asked him if he would provide the meats for the new restaurant and spoke of how he was so glad that all of the family could be involved in the business. He then asked Carmine—with his permission only—if

I could work in the restaurant two nights a week. He explained that with AnnaMaria there, the baby would be looked after and that the man really wanted my talents for dessert-making in the restaurant. The man—so my father said—had been all over the world and was convinced that no dessert had come close to the ones I created. He wondered respectfully if Carmine would allow me to work in the restaurant—for pay, of course—so that it could have the best dessert menu in town, maybe in all of New York. When I heard my father speak these words I felt my heart burst. I held my breath waiting for Carmine to answer. AnnaMaria sat quietly listening, and I could feel her wanting him to say *yes* as much as I did. She knew me as a child and knew that the woman I had become was not that same person. And she would love to have Donato to care for all by herself. To my greatest relief, Carmine agreed. He loved my father, and maybe that is why he found it hard to refuse him. Or maybe his heart was just ready to pass by his old hard beliefs that were limiting me…limiting us.

I started working on Thursday and Friday nights. Carmine often stayed late at the butcher shop on Fridays, cleaning up and taking weekend orders, so he agreed this would be less of a disruption to our life. AnnaMaria enjoyed having the baby all to herself and attempted to prepare meals on Thursdays for her, Carmine, and Donato. AnnaMaria was not a particularly good cook, so when I suggested that Carmine meet me at the restaurant on Thursdays so we could have dinner together when I was on break, he was so happy. In all the years we had been married, I had not made any attempt to make time for us to be together. Of course, I went along with whatever he wanted. I was a dutiful and obedient wife, but he could sense I could take or leave whether he was there or not. My work at the restaurant seemed to open me up. I became appreciative of him and my life. I found happiness inside me I had not felt in years, and because of this I was more pleasant, more open and ready to share myself with him. For the first time since we were married, we laughed together. I felt as if I was seeing him for the first time and like I actually liked him—maybe even fell in love with him. My work and my life started to fit, and I began to feel whole and complete. It was such a great feeling.

As the years went on, my father and the man opened many more restaurants. My parents' wealth grew, yet they remained simple, still living in Brooklyn. In 1950, they returned to Italy for a visit. We all went: my brother and his family, Carmine and I, and our three children and their families. We returned to my grandparents' village—our village—and to the place where our house once was. I was overwhelmed by how I felt and made peace with the fact that this place was now a destination but no longer my home. My home was in America. My mother passed away while we were there. She never really accepted America or the American ways as her home. I think she was so glad to be back she did not want to leave. We buried her next to her parents. By this time my brother ran most of the restaurants. My father still went to work every day even though he no longer needed to. We encouraged him to travel and enjoy life, but like me, his enjoyment came from working in the restaurant, being with the customers, and overseeing everything. I continued to work in the kitchen, staying with the original restaurant—only working in the others when a fire closed us down for several months. In the beginning I took the bus to work, but in 1942, when I was forty-five years old, I got my driver's license and Carmine bought me a car so I could get back and forth to work. He eventually let me work more, realizing I was a much better person to be around when I was doing what I loved. I was always careful to never allow my work to interfere with my family. And our marriage greatly improved after I started working. I was a much more loving and attentive wife to Carmine, and a better partner. I never really learned to enjoy the physical part of our relationship; I didn't hate it, but it was just not my cup of tea. After I passed I came to realize that in that life as Anna Vincenza, I was more physically attracted to women. It was neither something that never crossed my mind nor something I would have explored, but certainly there are other lives to live and other chances to fulfill that part of myself.

After my death, I understood that my life as Anna Vincenza was an authentically lived and fulfilling life. My soul found a way to express its creativity and purpose in a time when there was not a lot of freedom for women. My father and husband were very instrumental in bringing this forward, and I am blessed to have had them with me on that journey. Their love for me and their inner wisdom freed them from doing what they wanted and allowed me to be free. We all benefited from that, and our world and relationships became a better place for it. I know things are much different for you now in your modern world; most women have much more freedom now, although not in every part of your world. I like to believe I have contributed to this reality for you and that my humble family helped in some way. Living within your purpose truly creates joy, and then life flows so much easier. I do hope this message will help you all to understand how very simple it is. It has been my pleasure visiting with you today.

—Anna Vincenza

*

While writing this story I felt transported in time. I could hear the noises and smell the scents of Ellis Island and those Manhattan streets. I felt like I was there with her. This is known as remote viewing or astral travel. Remote viewing allows one to see a place or situation through the intuitive sense of clairvoyance, without directly experiencing it. It is like watching a movie. Astral travel is the sensation of being out of the body and traveling, some say like flying without a plane. I felt transported to Anna's timeframe and world and was experiencing it as she was describing it.

My grandparents came through Ellis Island around that time, and I never fully appreciated what it must have been like for them until reading Anna Vincenza's story. I certainly have much more gratitude for their efforts after reading this account. What tremendous courage and commitment it must have taken for all those who ventured away from family and familiarity. They were true pioneers who allowed future generations unforeseen opportunities. Those of us from these ancestral lines carry this pioneer energy in our own spiritual DNA. In present day, it is being activated within us so that we may break collective patterns and consciousness that limit, restrict, or otherwise oppress anyone. We are now being called to spiritually pioneer a world filled with peace, love, freedom, and equality.

In many ways, Anna Vincenza ventured far from the norm or expected in her lifetime. She was a true pioneer of a movement that would not be seen until the late 1960s and 1970s. Yet she did not realize the ground she was breaking—the patterns she was changing for future generations and for women in general. One life builds upon another, and all lives are connected. What we do in one lifetime in words, deeds, actions, and thoughts affects everyone—past, present, and future. Her father and husband managed to transcend a consciousness and belief system that made women subservient. This consciousness was a pattern, habit, and tradition of theirs, as well as the collective of that timeframe. The love they had (and still have) for her helped them to transcend the norm and step away from their own personal limits, and because of this, they changed all of their destinies. They all benefited from this...*we* all benefited from this. When love expanded within them, peace and harmony filled their relationships and lives. In many places on earth now, our reality includes a greater sense of equality, and this comes from the pioneers like Anna and her family who dared to break from tradition and follow their heart and inner guidance. Thank you, Anna, dear father, and Carmine. I, for one, am very grateful. Very well done!

—Ro, written June 7, 2012

4
LENNY

A Life Worth Living

As I sit in my writing room, I feel the excitement and readiness of spirit eager to connect with me. I try to anticipate who will come through and what they will share, but no matter what I imagine, the story is always better and more profound than I could ever conjure in my own mind. The plans are laid and set—there is a progression to these stories now coming into book form. As spirit anticipates the birth of this book into this world, the collective consciousness is being prepared to receive this information, this love, and this energetic gift. Lines are forming as those in spirit wait to share their stories with me. It's like the word has gotten out and they are eager to speak their truth and help us. As I sit in the power, I become aware of an energy presence. It is clear and strong. He does not waste any time as he begins to take me through his life. The images begin to form in my mind. At the same time, my family is here: my father and his brothers—my uncles. They are still and quiet and have with them a young boy named Lenny. As Lenny comes forward he changes from a sullen boy to his spiritual vibration or higher self. I soon realize it is Lenny's presence and images I was receiving. I was sensing him as a man, but he was with my father and uncles as a boy.

*

He begins to show me memories from his life even before he speaks. I start to get flashes in my mind, almost like my own memories, but I know they are not mine. I am linked to his mind and consciousness, and he shows me his thoughts as if he is thinking back, remembering, and I am witnessing or reviewing it with him. He is in the street playing kickball, and there is a fire hydrant spewing water into the curb. Children are running through it. He is in a very dirty white T-shirt and shorts that are too big. They are dirty too, like he has been wearing them for days. His mother sits on the stoop with a baby girl in her arms. She is sweating and fanning herself and wears a rag on her head. She is yelling for her children, giving instructions and orders. She is loving and strong as a mom but weak and indecisive as a woman. Lenny adores his mother. He is her oldest child and her protector. He conveys he stepped in front of many beatings for her. He is allowed to play after he finishes any chores he is told to do—and after he works at the corner bodega. Today he is playing kickball with Carl and Sergio. They still go to school—Lenny does not. They alternate playing kickball and running through the fire hydrant. They mess with the younger kids' games—everyone scatters when the trucks come barreling down the street. He shows me what it is like in the apartment: hot, humid, smelly, on the eighth floor of the Bronx walk-up. There is an image of him sitting frightened and still at the dinner table, with his sister to his right and the baby in the highchair Mrs. Wells left for them—she is from what's now known as social services. His mother making pancakes even though it is dinnertime. His father with his head buried in a plate that includes cheap sausages, eating away, not looking up—eating his pancakes with a tallboy beer. No one speaks. It feels like no one is even breathing—except the father. And the first words I hear Lenny speak in my mind are: *You never know what might set him off.*

We are now at the window of the apartment. The window is cold and he presses his face to it—so sad, so despairing. He's looking out, hearing the noise in the street...some sort of celebration—Christmas or New Year's—not in the apartment though. He tells me this is 1963, and it is almost a year after his mother has died. He says they were told she fell down the stairs and hit her head, but he knows it was three days after her last beating at the hands of his father that she fainted and the super had to call 911. He last saw her leaving in the ambulance with an oxygen mask on her face.

Lenny speaks:

It has been very hard since she left.... My stomach is constantly empty and agitated with fear. The lady next door minds my sisters a lot, but she is creepy—really creepy with me. I stay out of the house most of the day, looking to work in any way I can to make money to buy food or for food itself. The bodega man sends me home with all the old stuff too—it helps. My father shows up sometimes, when the welfare check comes, and then he is gone. We are more afraid when he is here. The apartment stinks real bad now...and there is no more pancakes. Right after the new year, Children's Advocacy shows up at our place. I try and tell them my father is at the store, but they know. Someone called them. I think it was that Nancy...she saw me walking on the street with a dirty T-shirt and no jacket and no socks when it was really, really cold. We were split up after that. I ended up in Englewood, New Jersey, with a family. Their names were the Holowells. They were very nice and made me wear socks all the time—and jackets too. My sister was sent to a family upstate. The baby...we never saw her again. After a year she was adopted by her fosters; my dad signed us away almost immediately after we were taken away. I think about that apartment in the Bronx, how dirty, how despairing, how dangerous it was, yet still, even as an adult, I miss it. I miss my mother and sisters and even the life I had there. To me, it wasn't bad.

I stayed with the Holowells into my teens. Mr. H got sick and I had to be placed with another family. Because Mrs. H was savvy and knew how the system worked, she made sure I was placed with a family in my vicinity—made sure I didn't have to change schools and start completely over. She put in place lots of things to ensure I would have an advantage in my new circumstances. She looked out for me and took care of me. I am very grateful for that. The family that took me in in my junior year of high school was the Favres. They were…different. I was provided for there but did not feel part of their life. Maybe that was my fault as I knew I would leave after high school and did not want to get too close.

When I first went back to school it was hard. I was way behind having not been in school for three years, but the Holowells got me a tutor—paid for it with their own money, not with the money the agency gave them. At first, I hated that they pushed me and made me do *extra* schoolwork, but then when I saw how others' looked at me because of my grades—because of my smarts—I didn't mind. After a while I didn't need the tutors; in fact, at times I knew more than them, especially in math. By the time I was with the Favres I was in all the advanced classes, and still they did not challenge me. No one talked to me about college though. It was known in the school that I was a foster, so it was assumed I would not have the means to go to college. At eighteen, you're on your own in the foster world. One lady, an aid in our school for a crippled kid, talked to me about my plans after high school. She didn't know anything about scholarships, but she knew that there was aid that may help me. She gave me some information, and I called Mrs. Holowell to see if she knew anything about this stuff. She didn't, but she got right on it, did some research, and gave me all the information in the fall of my senior year. She did all this while Mr. H was dying, right there in the house, with only her taking care of him.

Columbia was an interesting experience. I was on my own with a full ride. It wasn't called tuition aid or financial assistance then, and it wasn't considered a scholarship. It was an allotment, like a lottery, almost, that the school awarded to someone in need—considered a "give-back" or charity. It was through the school itself, and only three were awarded each year. You had to be extremely worthy—it was not a risk taken lightly by the administration. I lived and worked on campus full-time and studied biochemistry. I graduated in 1975, valedictorian of my class, and went on to Columbia medical school. Neuroscience became my thing. I invited Mrs. H to my graduation. She sat in the audience, very pleased with both me and herself. Afterwards she took me to lunch at 21. Medical school was harder for me—not academically—socially. Everyone was very competitive, and somehow everyone knew I was a foster kid who got charity to go to school. Would that ever leave me? Even though I worked hard and could hold my own in study, I was somehow disregarded because of where I came from. Most of my contemporaries were from very wealthy and accomplished families. Some were becoming doctors because everyone in their families was doctors. I was becoming a doctor because I *wanted* to be doctor. I was friends with a guy named Martin Harris lll. He took me to his family's home in Connecticut one weekend. He was always so self-assured, confident, and even funny at school, but as soon as we got to his parents' mansion, his whole demeanor changed. He became indecisive, timid, and defensive. He even stuttered. I realized then, that it doesn't matter where you come from or what you experienced—it's up to you to overcome whatever is inside you that holds you back.

I became a prominent neurosurgeon in New York City and met my wife, Helena, in our third year of residency. She is a noted psychiatrist, and we had a very good and supportive marriage that produced two wonderful children. I was killed crossing Amsterdam Ave. in 1996. I was killed instantly and never felt a thing. As I left my body, my mother was there. There was no rag on her head, and she was thin and beautiful. She was as I remembered her—only better. She hugged me, and I could smell her, and it was as if we were never separated.

My father came next, and he hugged me. It was like I was meeting him—the real him—for the first time. But I knew him; I could see him even though this was not the version I experienced on earth when I was alive. There was an overwhelming sense of love between us, and it was as if any hardship, fear, or strain that had existed between us never was. There were many people after that—patients, friends from childhood that I didn't even know that were dead, my grandparents who I had never met, and Mr. and Mrs. H. She was again pleased with me and herself for showing up. And it was all so…loving—that is the only word that you people would understand about this, but it was so much more. I looked at the life I had just left and felt so complete and so full; there was no sadness, no remorse, and no regret. I had a wonderful life, and every experience was blessed and cherished. I went on to live who I was supposed to be and what I was to become. I experienced everything I was supposed to.

My wife and children are still alive—my son now a doctor as well. I want to thank them for being part of my life and for all that we experienced together. I wait to greet them—until they can "see" me again. And I wait for my sisters as well. We will all see each other again. I know this for sure.

My name is Dr. Lennard Simacysk, and it was my pleasure to meet with you today.

*

After I wrote this, I waited a day to reread it. I thought I might have to reconnect to Lennard to add to his story. It was interesting to do that—to call in his energy. We read it together, and he only added one or two more retorts. He did not feel he needed to say any more. And as I read it, I realized it was simple and clear—just like him!

In my first moments of connecting to Lenny, I followed and described how he first led me through pictures and images and then, when he was ready to speak, through his dialogue. As I took dictation, I could hear his voice change from a child to a man. After his physical passing, his voice moved back to the innocence of the child he was, with the wisdom and understanding of the man he became. Lenny's story shows us that no matter what our life circumstances, we can still find a way to fulfill our destiny. He proves we can overcome any obstacle and remain true to our soul's plan. I love that he did not build any bitterness or resentment due to his experiences. He did not waste his energy blaming or being angry with his parents. Not only does this show great emotional maturity and intelligence, it speaks of a spirit determined to live authentically no matter what. He did not resist his circumstances; instead, he embraced every opportunity that was sent his way. I believe The Hollowells were his earth angels sent to assist him in staying on his path—and that their relationship was a collaboration made in spirit before any of them were born on earth. The Hollowells agreed to be there for him should he need assistance in this life to help him stay true to his course. I believe we all get such graces in our lives and that they are written into our scripts or soul plan. At times, we act as these graces for others.

His post-death meeting with his parents shows that our core connection is always love. Sometimes we lose ourselves while on earth, and with that we lose our connection to others. Sometimes it seems our actions make it harder to be loved or for us to give love, but this is just a mirror to the fact that we are not loving ourselves. It is through forgiveness and acceptance of the self and the return to love that heals all relationships and life traumas. It is love that we all seek. I hope Lenny's story encourages all of us to live true to our destiny and to release any excuse to live less than we are supposed to, no matter what the conditions are.

—Ro, written September 11, 2012

5
NANCY

Every Soul Has a Destiny

When I have worries, it takes me a while to get clear enough to "listen." My worries, like everyone else's, are just ego distractions—fears that sometimes keep me from being aligned with divine spirit and my own spirit and inner wisdom. It wastes my precious energy and keeps me separated and in the dark. It does not matter if the worries are justifiable. It is a mindset that can take over and disrupt my inner peace. Worry energy is dense, heavy, and despairing, and it sucks the life force out of you. Connecting to spirit is blissful and light, peaceful, calm, and powerful. Yet we humans are vulnerable to the tricks of our own mind and ego. I notice this today. And so I sit and observe all that is going on inside my mind instead of resisting it. Underneath the worry is a feeling of powerlessness and confusion. Soon I notice another part of my mind that speaks softly and quietly, and this part says to me, "None of this matters. Everything is exactly as it should be." Like a spell broken, the energy lifts, the worry shifts, and I begin to feel clear. As my mind empties into stillness and quiet, I enter that state of peace. My energy expands, my heart opens, I can't remember what I was worried about, and then, I am connected—to myself and to the divine power of spirit. How miraculous.

*

A woman comes and touches my left shoulder. Her touch is so gentle, so loving, as if she is someone I have known—someone from my own family. She assures me she is not but that the love and compassion she sends me now is as real and as powerful, as if it came from my own mother. Her name is Nancy and she was a nurse when she was alive. She comes from Dayton, Ohio, and was one of six children. She was the third eldest. She says her family was Irish-Catholic and that her father was a factory worker. Her mom was a stay-at-home mom, and she grew up in the 1950s.

Nancy speaks:

I was born in 1942 and went to school at Wilson Elementary in Dayton. I always wanted to be a nurse from the time I was a little girl. My brother broke his arm when he was twelve, and I remember tending to it until we got to the doctor. I insisted on staying with him, holding him, caring for him when he was in the office and the doctor was setting his bones. I was eight years old, and my mother kept trying to pry me from the room, but I insisted. He wanted me there also, and when the doctor saw how much comfort it gave my brother for me to be there, he let me stay. I didn't wince when they held him down and reset his arm. I held his other hand and looked into his eyes to keep him focused on me and not the procedure. It worked and he stayed steady—just allowing one single tear to run from the corner of his eye. I knew it hurt him, but he was able to stay with me. I held his focus, and that helped. When we got home he was very tired, but I was energized and spent the next week taking care of him as he lay in bed. My parents thought it was so sweet, but I felt it was my duty— my calling—and I never felt more alive. Of course I didn't know all of this in my eight-year-old mind, but I felt it in my heart and soul.

When I graduated high school I went right to Dayton School of Nursing. I finished in the required two years but was practicing my nursing skills long before I graduated. If anyone in the neighborhood was sick or ailing, I tended to them. I felt I already knew what I was learning through nursing school, like it was somehow in my mind and I was just remembering it. I breezed through school—it was easy and I excelled in every part, except for the surgical piece. I didn't like that—had a serious aversion to the OR procedures. I didn't mind the emergency room—which sometimes included emergency surgery—but for some reason, I did not like the OR rotation, the operating rooms, or most of the surgeons.

I began working at Memorial Hospital in 1962. I wore a typical white dress uniform with a nurse's hat. I thought it was very impractical, and I am so glad to see how things have changed since then. We never wore gloves—not realizing it was necessary for us or patients—and only wore masks when a patient had TB. How things have changed. Doctors were not always considerate or cooperative with the nursing staff—that hasn't changed much. However, every once in a while you would get a doctor that honored and respected the work the nurses did. One such man was Dr. Melman. He was an elder GP, and he treated the young and old. He counseled women on hygiene and reproduction when such things were not discussed. He performed abortions and felt very strongly that women had the right to choose their paths. I know this pained him, as his religion did not advocate such thoughts or actions, but somehow he managed to put that aside to tend to his patients in their time of need—and to the best of his ability. He was the most compassionate person I had ever met. I began to work with him closely in my fifth year as a nurse. I was on a general admissions floor, but he often sent patients to my floor under the guise of some other illness, knowing I would administer to their real needs. I was always careful to maintain the dignity and secret of my patient—not for my own sake but for theirs. Sometimes, their own family members—their own husbands—didn't even know the real reason they were there. There was Mrs. Smith (her name has been changed to keep her identity) who had four children under the age of five. She suffered tremendously from postpartum depression—something that was not understood or diagnosed at that time. She had no close family, and her husband traveled for business frequently. When she visited Dr. Melman for her fifth pregnancy, she burst into hysterics—threatening to kill herself and her children. Dr. Melman knew these were not idle threats and could see the desperation in this woman. He knew that it in fact would be dangerous and negligent to let her leave his office. He spent the next hour or so counseling her, and when he was sure she was clear—and adamant that she did not want, nor could handle another pregnancy, another child—he had her admitted to hospital under the guise of exhaustion due to food poisoning. In the early morning the next day, I met him at the hospital and he performed the abortion that probably saved that mother and those children. Mrs. Smith spent four more days in the hospital, her children being cared for by neighbors. She was solemn and still but more at peace than I had ever seen her previously. Dr. Melman counseled her after that, offering her some information on how to prevent future pregnancies. She must have listened, because she did not get pregnant after that and went on to raise her four children into good citizens. She frequently visited Dr. Melman for advice and counseling, as well as for illness. He knew he helped her and helped her children that day, and this allowed him to do what he felt was necessary. Another thing happened after that incident: Mrs. Smith learned that it was okay to ask her neighbors for help when she needed it. I think this helped her to feel less alone and more connected to people around her. While she didn't do it often, it was nice to hear her mention this when she came to the office. I believe that experience was life-changing for Mrs. Smith and her children—in a very good way.

One time, a girl of fifteen came in with her mother. The mother claimed the girl had stomach cramps and was sure she had a demon in her. Dr. Melman examined the girl and found her to be three months pregnant. He intuitively knew to speak to the girl alone and not the mother. Always compassionate and nonjudgmental, Dr. Melman came to learn the pregnancy was a product of incest. Yes, those things happened back then and most of the time were not addressed and certainly not talked about. He could have reported it, but most likely it would have been her word against her father's, and who knows what would have happened to her for telling. She would have been made to have that child and would have been shamed for doing so. Dr. Melman admitted her for "further testing," against the father *and* the mother's objections. He performed the abortion, calling it an exploratory procedure, and then recommended the girl convalesce in an abbey in Michigan. He had an in with the nuns who ran this abbey, often sending patients who were too far along in their pregnancies there for help. These women would often give their babies up for adoption after their birth, and the nuns would help them get on their feet and return to their lives. The nuns knew what the doctor did, and many of them supported him—secretly—for his service. They had seen too many women give birth to children and the trauma and shame this legacy could leave. The girl managed to stay for a full year, convincing her parents that she was considering a monastic life. The father objected but was afraid to go against the authority of the church, and the girl managed to escape the hell of her life and move to the West Coast to start a new life. She often wrote Dr. Melman and thanked him for giving her a second chance.

There are many other stories I could share, all unique and moving. We—Dr. Melman and I—did this procedure before it was legal, knowing full well the ramifications of our actions, knowing the shame it could bring to us, our families, the hospital, and our communities if we were ever caught, knowing we could go to jail. We didn't care; we felt we were helping these women, and in fact, time proved this to be true. In 1972, when Roe v. Wade passed, we felt great relief—not for the fact that what we were doing was now legal, but for the fact that any woman that ever needed help in this way could now get it without being jeopardized, harmed, or punished. I can't even begin to tell you how many women we treated who were maimed, dehumanized, and traumatized by those unqualified to do this procedure. We witnessed many deaths and disfigurement, and much more psychological trauma than one should witness due to the illegality of this issue. The passing of this law relieved much of this, and for that, we were both grateful.

I do not regret any part I played in supporting these women, in helping these women, often when no one would or could. I am proud that Dr. Melman and I worked together—that he asked me to work with him on this very worthy cause. I am honored to have met these women and to have been there to the best of my ability for them.

I married in my late twenties. My husband, a surgeon, knew of the work I did with Dr. Melman and completely supported it. We were never able to have children, and that was very painful for us. I often felt all the unborn babies were my children and that it was my job—my honor—to help them. I felt it was partly their decision not to be born, and I was helping them fulfill their destiny. My husband and I often supported and assisted the nuns in the abbey, offering our services and monetary support for their good work. We never thought of adopting, instead feeling fulfilled in our role to this organization.

I passed in 1996 at the age of fifty-four. I died of liver complications from hepatitis C—an occupational hazard. My husband, Richard, still lives in a suburb outside of Dayton and still performs surgery. When I passed, many of my patients greeted me. I received a lifetime of love and compassion from them, a testament to all that I gave to them. I am at peace, and so are they.

Thank you for letting me share this story with you. May you have peace.

—Nancy

*

Nancy brings us a very controversial subject. Some wonder, does life begin at conception or birth? What I have discovered in my work as a medium is that every soul chooses when to enter into physical form. Each individual soul chooses its life plan and lifetime (span). In other words, every soul chooses when it will incarnate, how long it will incarnate for, and also when it will leave this earth realm. Some choose to come to earth in physical form for only a short amount of time. Some decide not to incarnate after a body has already been formed. This often results in the ending of that pregnancy or body, one way or another.

Since we are all connected, our lives intertwining with each other, it would be a collaboration of all the souls involved—mother, father, and potential child, before incarnation—that decides the destiny and life plan that will play out among them all. The soul of the unborn child decides whether to be born or not. The soul of the unborn child may connect or disconnect to the body at any time during the pregnancy or soon after birth. Most of our soul energy remains in the realm we call heaven or the astral planes, with just a small amount embodying physical form. The souls of babies that are stillborn or miscarried decide on this destiny. It is always the soul's choice to incarnate and for how long. There are many reasons for this. Sometimes it has to do with the right timing. Some complete their karma and destiny in a short period of time, possibly even before they are physically born. Some fulfill their purpose just by being conceived. And some fulfill their purpose through their death. There are many reasons a soul chooses this path, and all of them are perfect and divine. Even while we are alive, our souls (spirits) have the ability to leave our bodies—and do so frequently. In fact, we all leave our bodies every night as we sleep when we go into our dream state. We visit the astral planes. As a soul, we understand there is no wrong timing for death. Every life, no matter how short or long, no matter what the quality, is worth living. On a soul level we understand that every earth experience is perfect and divine. There is no right or wrong; there is nothing out of order. It is always as it should be. Our human minds may think or feel differently based on our belief systems and programming, but from our spirit and the soul perspective, there is no right or wrong, no judgment. The soul of Mrs. Smith's baby created an opportunity for healing and balance within the whole family. The soul of the child within the teen girl allowed her to be liberated from a life of torment and suffering. These souls had a very high level of soul power to take on such circumstances and create such profound shifts in their loved ones' lives. They followed their destiny—their life's plan—without being born. Nancy expressed to me that she felt she was assisting these unborn souls as much as she was assisting their mothers. She felt her life work was a service. Her connection to all of them was from a place of love, support, compassion, and non-judgment. Shouldn't we all aspire to come from this place of unconditional love?

—Ro, written October 9, 2012

Section Two

Stories of Love, Healing, and Forgiveness

6
LARRY

An Opening for Compassion

Larry first spoke to me as I was taking my morning walk. I thought he was saying Harry at first. It wasn't until I got home and sat to speak with him that he corrected me. Sometimes for me, exercise acts as sort of a moving meditation. One can get clear and inspired as the body releases its stress and tension. I knew I would sit to write this day, and I guess my mind was opening while I was exercising. He made the connection to my open mind but was patient when I explained I had no paper or pen in that moment. As soon as I finished my walk and returned home, I sat to write his story. We were both ready.

*

My name is Larry, not Harry. People were always doing that when I was alive too—I guess I look like a Harry. I was born in 1948 in the Bronx, New York. We lived in a thirteenth-story flat. I had two sisters. My mother and father were devout Jews. I could take or leave my religion, even though I grew up in a community that was only Jewish.

I remember my bar mitzvah. Everyone was celebrating and congratulating me, and all I could think about was the rabbi's son, Morris, and how adorable he was. Morris was three years older than me. I didn't realize I was homosexual, but I knew enough not to express these feelings. I grew and went to Fordham University—where all nice Jewish Bronx boys go, I guess, and I met a lovely girl named Marianne, and we married before I even finished my degree. I was a virgin and so was she. Thank God for that, because she did not realize how inept I was at sex with a woman. We had two beautiful daughters, Miriam and Bernadette, and we lived in the same neighborhood in the Bronx I had grown up in. We eventually moved to Westchester, and I excelled in my career. My work took me frequently into Manhattan, and I loved this. I especially loved when I had to go all the way Downtown, where it seemed no one knew me and where I was exposed to things I had not seen living all the way Uptown. It was like a new world.

One day I had a meeting with a client on the Lower East Side. I was an architect and was meeting a man who was very renowned in the arts…that is all I will say about him. I was to design the renovations for the new loft apartment he had recently purchased. We met at a restaurant on East 4th Street and Avenue A. It was very different from what I had ever experienced, and I chalked it up to the artisan-Bohemian lifestyle this man lived. He asked me if I dated, which I thought was odd coming from a man, and I told him I was married. He laughed hysterically at this, and I had no idea why that was so funny. He asked me if I knew what I was. This man was so confusing and yet so intriguing to me. I was not sure what he was talking about. We soon left the restaurant and went to a local bar. There were men dancing in cages and on a very small stage. There were men everywhere, and some were even kissing and doing other things in very dark corners. There was a lot of smoke, and some was not just cigarette smoke. There was so much going on at once; I could not take it all in. The man that brought me asked me what I thought of this place. I told him I was appalled, but he knew—and I knew—this was not true. I know I sound so completely naïve…I really wasn't; I knew what homosexuality was in concept. I was thirty-two years old. This was the first time I had seen it, and it was up close and very personal. The man grabbed my hand and asked me to dance. I tried to look shocked and resistant, but there was another part of me that gave way and just willingly walked with him to the middle of what was the dancing area. He led, of course, and laughed at my very perplexed expression. He handed me a drink of something and a pill. I accepted everything without any struggle. I was so removed from who I knew myself to be and from the life I had lived and experienced previous to this night—and I was not afraid or resistant. I complied completely with what this man offered.

That night was the first night I kissed a man. It was not the man who brought me. It was the man who walked me to the train station so I could return to Grand Central Station and my life upstate. The man who brought me introduced me to Stephen, and then he left with a very young—almost too young—man. This was the beginning of my life as a gay man—and also the beginning of the double life I led until my death.

Stephen introduced me to many things that I did not know existed. There was a whole subculture to this homosexuality thing. I was very drawn to the darker side of it, I must admit. I made any excuse I could to be out of the house and Downtown. There was a favorite bath house I visited on Amsterdam Ave. also. I was more alive than I had ever been. I was not afraid—I felt completely and utterly free and in control at the same time. I felt no one from my real life would ever suspect what I was doing—not even Marianne—and they didn't. Once, a young male colleague new to the office made an inquisitive face about someplace I mentioned I had visited. It was the only time anyone had ever made a homosexual connection to me; he realized the neighborhood this establishment was in and immediately put it together. He never said a word to me or anyone else, but we both knew he knew.

In 1987 I developed this serious cough. I could not shake it no matter how many rounds of antibiotics I took. After a few months I developed a rash on my body—red spots that started on my chest and torso and began moving up the back of my neck. My wife insisted I visit our family physician, Morty. She was sure he would be able to clear it right up. As soon as I took off my shirt, Morty knew exactly what I had. He volunteered at a clinic in East Harlem and had seen many cases of AIDS in recent years. This epidemic was just hitting its stride.

I, of course, clueless as ever, had no idea what he was referring to. There was talk in my secret circles of a disease that was devastating, but because of where these conversations were held, they were quickly dismissed and not discussed. My arrogance of my situation prevented me from ever fearing this would happen to me. It was not even a thought in my mind, even though my behaviors were exactly the reason this disease spread so rampantly. Morty was aghast at my situation. He refused to treat me and sent me to speak to a doctor at Columbia Presbyterian that specialized in this disease. I continued to lead my double life; I truly lived as if I were two different people, but the one common bond was that in neither life I lived like I was sick and dying. Call it denial, but I continued to live as if the situation was not happening and I was not sick. I told my wife that I had a skin infection and Morty gave me a cream. I continued to meet men and have anonymous sex. It was only if they saw me naked that they realized I may be sick. Most left; some stayed anyway. I continued to go to work, hacking away and getting thinner every day. The kid in my office who knew—suspected my secret—no longer worked there. He would have known immediately the signs if he was still there. I wonder what he would have done with that information. The man—the artist—who originally was my first contact to this life had passed away unexpectedly two years before. There had been rumors that he had the "gay cancer," but I never checked and never went to his funeral.

One day, at work, I collapsed. I was rushed to Roosevelt-St. Luke's.

They had a special floor for patients in my condition. The EMTs recognized what I had and immediately put on what looked like hazmat suits. My wife was called and met me at the hospital. I was not there when she was informed of what I had and that I was at end stage. I was in extreme isolation. No one came into that room without being covered from head to toe. My daughters wept uncontrollably by the door—I could see them through the window in the door. My wife never cried. She just looked confused and frightened. This did not add up in her mind, and she could not grasp what it all meant. My father, who was still living, came to the hospital. There was only one thing I had ever feared during this time in my life—that was my father finding out I liked men and that I had sex with men. When he looked through the door, I knew he knew. I expected to see repugnance and hate, but what I saw in my father's eyes—what I felt from him, even through the door—was compassion and his love for me. I was shocked. My father came almost every day. My wife came a lot and then slowly stopped coming. My daughters came once a week. None of my friends from either life came, none of my coworkers, neighbors, or lovers. Some did not know. Those who did shunned me and my family. I spent two and a half months in the hospital...mostly in isolation. I died one night when no one was there. I died alone.... This is how I always felt in my life. I did not feel remorse for anything—not for my choices and not for everyone finding out. I did not feel peace either. I felt neutral, as if none of it mattered—not my wife, my work, my family, my gay lifestyle, and my secrets...none of it.

After I passed, I did feel something. I felt a love for myself that I had never felt before. It was like the inside of me opened up and I could feel a love for myself—not the Larry self or husband-son-Jewish self, not the gay self—just love for my true self that included all of these parts. I was overcome with a sense of love inside. I then became aware of the deep and ever-present love that was surrounding me. I think it was always there—even while on earth when I was alive—but I never noticed and now I did. I let it embrace me, and I melted into it with the love that was within me.

I am very happy to say that through the death of me and others like me, there was a compassion shift on earth. I would love to think it started with my father, but I know it did not. We all have compassion inside of us, just like we have self-love. It sometimes takes an outside event to trigger it, wake it up, so to speak. AIDS and the death of so many beloved husbands, sons, fathers, best friends, as well as women and children, triggered a mass opening of compassion inside the heart of humanity. I am very grateful to have played my part.

With love to my family, I hope your suffering can end with this message.

—Larry

*

When I sit to write these stories, I have no idea what message will be conveyed, where the story will go, or what life experiences will be shared. Larry gave me his birth year—no one had mentioned that before. When I realized Larry was referring to the AIDS epidemic, I immediately wanted to check his birth year to see if it correlated to that time, but I couldn't seem to interrupt the flow of thought that he was directing to me. It was only after I finished and reread this story that I realized it completely aligned to that time in history. I was in my twenties when the AIDS crisis was top news. I worked in New York City and had many friends who were touched by AIDS. I knew of the fear, shame, and isolation that surrounded those who suffered through this disease, and I always thought of it as a very sad and fearful time in our collective past. I have no idea if there were bath houses on Amsterdam Ave. or where he was referring to as his Downtown haunts. That was a world that I did not have access to.

What I really like about Larry and his story is that he makes no apologies for his life or his choices. In fact, I believe even while he was living these choices and their consequences, he did not question them. Maybe these were not choices made from bad character or ego. Maybe choices, even when they seem immoral or selfish, are sometimes collaborations from the soul—made from a higher place of service. When he spoke of the AIDS epidemic being an opening in the heart of humanity, it instantly changed my whole perspective of that time. It changed my view of those who perished, from seeing them as victims who were shamed and ostracized to the perception that they somehow had a part in a greater plan that helped all of us grow and ascend to a higher level of consciousness. Maybe they were not victims but spiritual warriors who sacrificed so we could all be better beings. I am completely grateful to Larry and others like him who suffered so I might *get it.*

—Ro, written January 3, 2012

7

BABY EMILY

The Opportunity

I am waiting for a presence to enter my space today, but somehow the connection seems much more impersonal. There is no presence with me, but I do feel an energy shift that lets me know something is about to download. This is the third sitting I have had with spirit, and all have been different. I start to receive a "knowing" that connects to my mind. We refer to this as *claircognizance*. The information is not in my frame of reference. I wasn't aware that typhoid was spread by rodents. Afterwards, I investigate that possibility and confirm this was indeed true. I don't feel I "connected" to Emily or her mother, Hannah, but instead recited their experience from the spiritual perspective. In medium circles this is known as accessing information from the akashic records. The akashic records are described as containing all knowledge of human experience and the history of the cosmos. They are metaphorically described as a library, or universal supercomputer database or the "mind of God." Edgar Cayce, a renowned early twentieth-century psychic, medium, and healer often accessed the akashic records for people, giving them information on healing, often causing miraculous results. This was very different from the ways I had worked before, and as I would soon learn, every story would be brought to me in different ways.

*

In my inner vision, Father Padre Pio is holding a child—a little girl, infant. She was born in 1915 to a very wealthy family in England. The mother of this child, Hannah Bell, came to the US on a boat—post Titanic but just as big. The Atlantic? The Atlantic Voyager? She brought the three-month-old infant along; it was a pleasure trip. There was a Negro nanny along also. Her name was Pearl. The child was bitten by a rat on the cruise, and so was the Nanny. Both became violently ill with what seemed like typhoid fever. It was assumed the nanny made the child sick somehow. They were bitten in their sleep as the baby slept in the nanny's bed with her. Upon arriving to New York, the child was taken to the doctor. The nanny suffered terribly in isolation, blamed for the illness and shunned—what a precursor to the days of AIDS. The child was treated but to no avail. She passed within a week of landing in New York. The nanny was subsequently beaten and punished with no food and water, and in her very weakened state, passed soon after. She had no will to live anyway as she loved this child Emily like her very own. The nanny was only eighteen and would not have had the opportunity to have her own children.... On an intuitive level she knew this and poured her heart to this child with a mother's love. Emily loved her too and had a bond so complete with Pearl, that the mother, Hannah, often felt the tenseness of her own child as she held her in her arms. Perhaps the jealousy of this bond fueled the punishment and death of this very innocent woman. Emily appeared to Hannah in a dream some years later—she was a child of about four or five—the age she would have been if she had lived. She had loose, soft blond hair and a white lace dress on. She was smiling and happy—happy to see her mother, happy to hold her in the dream. She gave her mother a note to read—sort of a handmade card a child of her age would draw with crayons for a special occasion. She told her mother to read it when she left. Hannah focused so much on Emily—and trying to hold the experience—she forgot the card until months later, when an encounter with a similar little girl triggered the memory of the dream. She could not remember opening the card or what the card said. It was about that time that she began to wonder if the nanny had really caused her child's death. Now back in England, there had been an outbreak of typhoid, and the symptoms were very similar to Pearl's and Emily's. It was announced that rats were causing this outbreak and to avoid them at all cost. Still, to allow her mind to wonder, to find this truth, she would have had to take responsibility for taking her child on this trip; she would have had to take responsibility for the death and punishment of Pearl; she would have had to reopen and subsequently heal the wounds of the loss of her child and her broken heart. The opportunity was there. She did not take it. Instead, she buried it deeper in her core, burned all of the remaining remnants of Emily—pictures, belongings, mementos—and never spoke of her again. She put her out of her heart and didn't get a chance to experience her again until the day she passed and was greeted first and foremost by Emily and Pearl. Hannah's life, while full of beautiful possessions, children, love all around, was basically empty and hollow. Emily brought her the opportunity to heal. She could not take it.

*

Father Padre Pio was a Catholic priest from Italy who died in 1968. He was famous for having the stigmata and for his mystical experiences to receive visions, to bi-locate, and to perform miracles. He was canonized in 2002. Father Padre Pio was sickly most of his life. He believed his physical suffering was his path to the deepest connection to God. Through his suffering, he held that his heart and the heart of God merged. It is said he dedicated his life to aid those who suffered, and he performed many miracles to ease physical illness and pain.

What I didn't know was that Father Padre Pio had suffered typhoid as a ten-year-old child.

We don't always know how disease is spread. In our grief it is easy to move into anger and blame. As Emily connected to Hannah's mind and heart from spirit, Hannah had an awakening. This awakening offered Hannah a way past her suffering, but this would have required her to face her mistake and forgive herself. Spirit and our loved ones who have passed often create opportunities for us to heal and grow past our pain. We are often given chances to open our hearts and find the love that is there. As demonstrated in this story, we do not always take them. But they will keep returning; we never run out of chances, as spirit's main goal is to always allow us a chance to return to love, to return to peace, and to make peace with all of our life experiences.

—Ro, written October 19, 2010

8
THOMAS

Visits from the Other Side

Thomas came into the living room and sat on my couch. He began speaking to me face to face. He came as a little boy, but like many of the others, there was a wisdom and clarity in his communication beyond his physical life years. He told me details of his life and death and answered unspoken questions as if he were reading my mind. This is known as telepathic communication.

We are all telepathic beings. We all have the ability to communicate telepathically with those living as well as with those who have passed. When spirits communicate through thoughts or telepathy, it is referred to as mental mediumship. Mediums develop the ability to discern their own thoughts from those they receive through mediumship. This training is done through meditation, awareness, and mediumship practices.

The practice of meditation allows one to connect with the aware mind or the *self* that bears witness. Through meditation, we learn to observe our thoughts instead of identifying with them. When one develops their mediumistic ability, they learn to open the mind, to separate and witness thoughts, and also to raise the energetic vibration so a connection can be made to the presence of the spirit world. As we hold this connection, we can then receive information through words, pictures, images, thoughts, physical sensations, and symbols. The meditation practice allows the medium to know which thoughts come from the medium and which are being received through the mental portal of the medium. Meditation does not make everyone a medium, but I believe we all have the ability to hear and connect to our own loved ones in spirit, and meditating can help facilitate this process by opening and calming the mind.

Authentic connection to the spirit world includes "evidence" or "evidential information" that allows the sitter to know the medium has indeed connected to their loved one. Evidence can include gender, timeframes, age and cause of death, personality traits, lifestyle information, dates, geography, names, specific life events, and connection—such as mother, father, son, daughter. Those in spirit know that people on earth need this sort of description to recognize and connect with their energy and essence. Once that connection is confirmed between the medium, the sitter, and the spirit coming through, the energy opens, flows, and merges to form a very powerful and moving experience. A portal is then created where divinity showers love, healing, and compassion to everyone present. In these moments, the illusion of separation is suspended, and love and peace prevail.

On this day, Thomas opens that portal to me.

*

I was only here a short time—on earth I mean. I was two years and three months when I perished. It was in a fire; my parents could not get to me. I was sleeping in my crib when the flames ignited. I was not afraid, as I was asleep. I was dreaming, I guess, and there was a beautiful woman who looked as sweet as my mother. I remember her lifting me from my crib and cradling me; I felt so safe, so loved. She was so beautiful and comforting. She told me it was time to come with her now—my time was done—and she lifted me to a place far away from my home, my room, my mum. I was not sad or afraid, and I never felt any pain. I just knew it was all right and that my mom and dad would be all right. I returned to the magical garden that is reserved for the young. I play with the other children, even though many have already begun a new endeavor—what you would call a new life. We often return to the earth realm to check in on our families, as we know our passing causes them so much heartache and grief. We try as best as we can to let them know we are there and to comfort them. One boy taught me how to wrap my arms—which are now only love and no longer physical—around my mom's body so she may feel me. She thinks she is thinking of me, remembering holding me when I was with her on earth, but it is really me holding her from this realm. It feels so nice, and for an instant, we are together and feel the same thing: intense love and connection. She often gets busy soon after that happens, almost to brush it away…but I stay for a while, looking for the opportunity to do it again. Sometimes I go with my friend Cal to visit his family on earth. His brother can "see" us in his mind. His mum thinks that he is imagining us—that he misses Cal and has made up me with Cal. He insists that Thomas is here as well, but she remains baffled. We didn't know each other on earth—Cal and me—but we would have if we had grown. Our paths would have crossed in our nineteenth year of life. We would have been college roommates in Cambridge. He had an older brother, Steven, and a younger sister, Madeline, who they call Maddie. He passed of a genetic disease that his siblings do not possess. We often assist each other when visiting earth—it makes the energy stronger and more noticeable—and besides, we have so much fun doing this. People wonder what happens when children die. The answer is not simple. Some just return to the realm of spirit and wait for instruction to return to form. Others join energy and offer energy vibration of pure love to specific places on earth or any part of the cosmos, really. We all retain the imprint of the life we had just lived until the parents who brought us to earth leave that realm and their form. In other words, when our earth parents cease to exist on earth, so does the form we took on. From earth this is a little hard to understand. The form shifts even though the memory or energy fragment still remains. Enough of that. Do you think my mum and dad will read this? It has been a while since I passed from earth. They have since moved to a suburb outside of Manchester, named Mansfield Landing. They have a new daughter: Elizabeth, after the queen. I helped bring her to earth—was with her when she left spirit in her descent into body. She remembers me, not only through my parents' musings about me, but also because I am always with her.

I experience her life as if it were mine. Only one of us would have been there, and she would have experienced life through me if things had been different. She is almost twelve now—a beautiful girl who has put the love and joy back into my parents' hearts. I still go and wrap my arms around mum every once in a while; I will do that until she meets me here. Please tell my parents I love them and I am with them always in heart and when they think of me—I am with them completely. Oh, and tell them I am glad they did not name me Stewart!

*

This story is very detailed in its evidence, not only about Thomas the speaker, but also the information he provides about his friend Cal whom he met in spirit. It gave me great comfort to know Thomas did not suffer and was protected during his final moments on earth. I believe this experience is common to those who pass tragically and abruptly and that the only suffering is for those living who relive the trauma in their mind.

Thomas gives very clear information about how those from spirit continuously reach to connect to those living on earth and how this is energetically done. He offers specific details about what happens to children who have passed and how they live in spirit. More importantly, he clearly shows that a medium is not needed for those from spirit to connect to their earth living loved ones. They can come at any time, and they often do. Our logical mind and our wounded and grieving heart sometimes prevent us from acknowledging this, and yet, our energy body responds and our minds receive the telepathic connection.

Perhaps Thomas's account and explanation of how spirit visits us will help us to acknowledge and accept these visits filled with love. I hope this brings peace and comfort to others as it has to me.

—Ro, written February 9, 2011

9

JOSELF

The Power of Love to Heal and Transform

By the time I sat to write Joself's story, I was much more comfortable with the process. Spirit and I had formed a routine, and I knew what my role was in all of this work. My preparation began. I would sit, light a candle, meditate a bit, and then receive the information...but this story was different. As Joself described his life circumstance, I began to get uncomfortable and emotional. My heart hurt and I cried as I sympathized with his fate. I connected from a mother's heart and instinct instead of the medium part of me that can remain compassionately detached. It was too much to bear. Why would spirit deliver such a heartbreaking story? I resisted. At first I tried to intervene and change the direction of his story to one before his life-altering event, but I couldn't. Finally, halfway through, I just stopped writing. I began arguing with spirit that this story was too disturbing—too painful to be included with these other uplifting and loving stories. Besides, I was too emotional and disturbed to be clear. My intention was to just leave it unfinished.

For about two weeks, I was able to put it out of my mind. Spirit then began to encourage me to revisit this story. I didn't know if I could reconnect to Joself now that I had severed the original connection. One day, I decided to sit and open the story. Joself immediately showed up, and we picked up exactly where we had left off. In my mind, I stayed as open and receptive as I could. I let the story flow from my fingers without any emotional attachment, judgment, or question. I am still amazed at the inspirational and revealing message that finally came through Joself's narrations. I am very grateful I returned to this story, and I am honored to reveal such powerful information here.

*

I have the energy of a small child trying to connect to me. He is not in the room, rather, connecting directly to my consciousness. He is about five or six years old, and even though he is a child I feel the wisdom of his soul. He is imprinting images in my mind about him and three other small children. He is the oldest. One is just an infant. They seem to be orphans—abandoned. He says their parents were taken away in a raid. The year is 1931. This is Russia—or a part of it. Their village was decimated by a government regime. The adults and children twelve and older were taken prisoner. The young children were left there to fend for themselves. Most are just huddling in burned or abandoned homes and shops. They are confused, disoriented, and dazed. They are not harmed…just left. The energy of this place feels thick with grief and incomprehension. Wails of parents being torn from their children echo in the dead silence of this place. This boy named Joself describes the chaos of the invasion—how military forces came in and made everyone get out of their homes and businesses and step into the street. While they were held, other military men went into the places to search for those hiding and also to search for anything valuable. It was a poor village, so there was not much in the way of valuables. Anyone found hiding was shot on the spot. As those in the street heard this, they began to resist…. Some of those people were shot as well….

Joself speaks:

Mayhem began, and then the next thing, the adults were rounded up into trucks and driven away as we, the younger children, were left in the street. Most of the adults were later executed…some interned…. They all eventually die and never return. I am one of the oldest left here. We naturally gravitate towards each other—the children—and try and stay in one place waiting for the parents to come get us. We wait a very long time; most everyone is crying. As it starts to get dark and we begin to get afraid, we go into the nearest house. None of us know how to turn the lights on. We sit in the dark. Some of us look for food in the pantry. There is some bread and milk in the icebox. There are no bottles. One of the girls is holding an infant that was left behind. I think it is her sister. We hold the milk bottle to the baby's mouth, but she or he does not know how to drink from there. The milk spills on the floor, and the baby, soaking wet from the milk, is wailing. We try and see if he or she can eat some bread. This just makes it choke. We give up and huddle together, alone, afraid, hungry, and cold. I sleep on and off, waking with every sound, hoping it is my mother and father returning for me. The next morning when it is light out, we walk outside again and wait in the street… not wanting the owner of the home to be angry with us for intruding on their house. We wait in the street, looking in the direction where our families left. At night we retreat into another home and huddle together the same way, waiting for the morning light. By the third day, the baby is no longer crying and barely moving. I come to find he is a boy, and his sister, who is only four, is holding on to him dearly. We begin to speak with some of the others—some cry, some are angry. The oldest here is eight years old, but no one listens to her as she seems more confused and helpless than the rest of us. I decide we must go to the grocer in the center of the village to get some food and water. There is a pump and well there that we can reach. Some of the houses do not have running water—the ones that do, we have a hard time reaching the sink.

We walk together, all the while watching the road for signs of their return. We go into the store and find crackers and milk, some fruit too, and potatoes, but they do not taste good raw. There is meat in the case, but again, it is raw and we cannot cook it. Some of it smells as if it is starting to rot. We take some of the food, milk, and a bucket of water back to where we're left standing. As we are walking back, I see my house and go into it. I thought maybe someone might have returned without me seeing and that maybe they would be waiting for me. There is emptiness and silence; coffee on the table, cold; and my father's cigarette burned to the end with a trail of white ashes—just sitting there. I want to stay in here and I can't—can't bear to be in the house by myself in all of this silence. It is better to be in the street here; they can see us, I think. I wipe away my tears so the others do not see—they would be afraid to see me cry. They have come to think of me as the leader. Days go by and we do the same thing: sit in the street and wait by day, take refuge at night in a home close by. Once we went into a home and smelled an awful smell. As we looked around, we found a body of a young teen girl and child. It was dark, so we could not see it well, but we knew what it was. We left quickly and went to another home, remembering never to go to that one again.

As the days passed, there began to be less and less of us. The baby had long died. The sister carried him for quite a while even when we knew he was dead. We finally convinced her to lay him in a garden in the back of someone's home. She worried what she would tell her parents when they returned. Would they be mad at her for not caring for her brother and letting him die? It bothered me that she was so worried about this, but I could not seem to comfort her. We grew dirtier and hungrier. We began to search the houses for food. We did this out of desperation and necessity. We were trying to stay alive so that we could see our parents again. Every day, there were less and less of us. Some just gave up their will to live, I think. Some just died in the street waiting for their parents—for anyone—to return.

I tell you this story because there are not many who knew this story. Our whole village was wiped out. We were just one of the many villages trampled by the regime. For a long time our village remained a ghost town. Many of us who died did not leave after physical death. We waited and wandered, hungry, cold, and tired. What had happened there was never addressed, acknowledged, or rectified. There was never a healing, and without a healing, we stayed stuck—the energy stayed stuck. The earth then carried the wound in the very ground there.

Since this had happened in many places in this area, it became a place where only tragedy prevailed. Any time something new was started in these places, somehow something bad would happen and people—and the light within them that they brought—would pull away. People knew of the terrible things that had happened in these parts. They had heard the history and remembered this as time of great despair and hate in this land at that time. We were acknowledged as "ghosts" who haunted these places and were blamed for the bad things that continued to occur—but it wasn't "us." It wasn't even the dark energy left there by the events, what you would call an "energy charge"; it was the calling out for a healing, a love, a peace. It was the energy asking to be released through the acknowledgment and power of love and forgiveness. If someone, anyone, who had come here stopped and remembered the story of the tragedy and spent one moment just filling their heart with love instead of filling their mind and heart with fear, the energy would have been broken. Almost like a spell or a curse being lifted, the energy, the earth, even the history and events would have been forever changed. The love would transform the place—and us—back into light. It is that simple. If many people did this, the effect would be so profound; it would affect the entire planet. You see, places that hold this much darkness are also the portal for great transformation and healing. It is in such places—and situations, I might add—that someone who has the ability to release their fears and step completely into the love in their heart will create a cataclysmic experience of love on this earth and literally change the ground we all walk on. And—it will create immunity to the dense negativity that will not be challenged. When most people encounter what they feel is negative, dark, dangerous, even confusing, they retreat, pull away, and move into fear perceptions, beliefs, and emotions. This feeds what is already there. If they remembered to stop and focus on love—to go past the moment and past the fears and feel the heart full of all the love inside—in an instant, everything would change. Can you tell them this for us? It is so simple.

Our spirits stayed in that earth space for quite a while. And then, one day, our parents in their spirit presence returned for us. The love they felt freed us to leave and go to what you refer to as heaven. Somehow, one or more broke their trauma by finding the love in their heart. This allowed the group to transcend and then ascend. We are all free now, but the space on earth is not. It needs the healing of love so that history does not continue to repeat itself—maybe not in the exact same way, but always with the exact same feeling. If you are reading this, please, spend one moment feeling all the love in your heart. Think of those you love, the moments in your life where you have felt great love, and when that feeling builds up inside of you, send it like a great ball of energy to this place. You do not need to know the exact location; your intent will direct it. By doing this, you are performing a great act of service that will change your world. It is the love in your heart that is needed. Please remember it is there.

My name is Joself. I was born in 1925 in a tiny village in southwest Russia. This is the story of what happened to those who fought tyranny and injustice at that time.

*

Joself's message of the heart is a very powerful practice we can all do. We just needed to be reminded. It is easy to succumb to fear. Fear is seductive and almost hypnotic; the energy of love is soft and gentle. Evil is of the physical world. Spirit—our spirit—is beyond this world. It feels natural to move away and resist that which feels negative or fearful, yet if we remember to stay connected to love, to embrace these feelings and forces from a place of love within, maybe we can transform our world and ourselves. Keeping our hearts open is the only answer, and when we do, we honor Joself and all those who have ever suffered and endured evil and injustice. We then transform that which creates evil and return to the natural and rightful state of love and peace.

—Ro, written September 27, 2010, to October 18, 2012

10

ERNIE

It's Never Too Late to Say I Am Sorry

Today I feel an excitement to connect with spirit and write a story. Recently, in a medium class I attended, an opportunity opened that allowed spirit to move much closer and to connect with me in a much deeper way than I have previously experienced. Just like in the movie *Ghost*, spirit embodied my energy field and used my physical presence to express itself. It is not that the spirit takes over or enters the physical body as much as the spirit uses the energy field of the medium to come through and take form. The presence of the deceased person is so strong and clear that the earth person receiving the communication feels as if their loved one is right there with them. The experience in class was extremely profound—even while observing other mediums do it. For those living, it feels like a reunion with a loved one. The medium's presence is not even felt, and it requires great surrender, trust, and allowance on the part of the medium.

The medium also needs a certain amount of soul stamina. Using the energy of the soul self allows for a complete merging with the soul (spirit) coming through. This energy can then be built, held, and developed, allowing for an extraordinary visit with our departed loved ones. If the medium's vibration drops or the soul power is not there, the connection fails.

As we practiced, I realized spirit has been embodying my energy when I do these writings, even though the writing comes through my mind. I don't feel "taken over"—more like I am deep inside myself and I am allowing someone else to use my body, mind, and energy to be present in the moment. This experience allows the spirit to communicate directly with their loved ones. My excitement and eagerness today is about being aware of this possibility. I can't wait to see what will happen. Suddenly, I feel an intense physical shift in my body. A whoosh of energy blasts through me, and I feel like a man—a large man with big hands and hairy knuckles....

*

I am a well-known writer, and you know me as a man named Ernest Hemingway. I lived in the early part of the twentieth century and wrote from my home. Frankly, I never saw the fuss in my work, but apparently many people liked it. I always thought my writing was a little outlandish and never, ever took myself too seriously as a writer. I was known to drink a bit and was fond of overeating food. Many people do not know that about me. I also really liked women and had many women in my lifetime. I had a hard time staying with one and was not faithful when I was. I lived my life by the seat of my pants most of the time, and contrary to what many people would suspect, I frequently had money problems—more specifically, I often lacked for enough money. When I did have money, I spent it foolishly and squandered a lot on bad investments and gambling. Considering I lived a life that looked very successful, and was much acclaimed, my greatest success was in the eyes of the universe. I was raised Presbyterian but never went to church much after my upbringing. I did dabble in the esoteric, not really finding a place there either. But I do believe what I wrote came from a place that was inspired beyond experience or imagination. I believe I was a channel (like you are now) for message and metaphor on how to live life—only my stories were not about how we do it well, but sometimes how we do it wrong. They must mean something, because they are still read and revered today. I would sometimes read back on my own work and wonder what the hell they meant or why people liked them so much. When I wasn't writing them, I had no connection to the work; they held no meaning to me. You would think someone like me would be the last person that spirit would use to deliver a message. It just goes to show you we are all capable of great things and that everyone on this earth has the potential for greatness. I want to use this space to speak to my own personal people—just like everyone else who has come to tell their story to you. I'd like to speak to Re, my daughter, whom I loved deeply but had a hard time relating or connecting to. I am sorry. For all the women who I loved (because I did love them in my own way—maybe not their way), I am sorry for any pain I caused you. This is for the women who have passed, and certainly for the remaining few who are alive. I was a bastard to you all at some point during our relations. It was my trademark, and I'd like to say I couldn't help myself, but I could have. I want to thank the lovely couple who ran the café I ate breakfast in every morning. It was a delight to see you all and be treated like family—not a celebrity. I liked that you did not put up with my shit and called me out when I was being surly or negative. I hated when people treated me differently and overlooked my nastiness. I respect you for all you have done and hope you appreciate the gift I left you—I know you do.

As for the person who found me after my death, I liked the little prayer you said over me—not my sort of thing, but it was appreciated. You also did not capitalize on the celebrity part and instead treated me with dignity and respect as a person, a fellow human being.

I am sorry I do not have any words of wisdom for the masses or any inspirations or epiphanies like your other stories. What I do have is a sincere appreciation for earth life, pleasure, and even hedonistic experiences, and I am sending that energy through these words for all that read them. May you enjoy your life experience as much as I did. May you make no apology for your life—responsibility for your actions, yes, but no apology for who you are, what you did or did not do, and for all you are: the good, the bad, the ugly, and the very good. Stay true to yourself and the rest is easy.

God bless you all,

Ernie

*

This presence is not subtle. As he moves out of my energy field, it feels as if my body has just deflated, and I am back to myself. It's not that I had left; it's more like I was tucked away inside and shared the space with him. My first thought was, *Did I just connect to THEE Ernest Hemingway?* I could hear him speak as if he was addressing an audience and was aware of his fingers typing on the keyboard—like I was observing all of this *and* experiencing him at the same time.

Funny, I don't know a thing about Ernest Hemingway; I can't even remember off the top of my head what he has written. I, a voracious reader, have never read any of his books or anything about him or his life. I guess that is a good thing, as I have no frame of reference to go by and no influence from his writings.

His connection to my energy was very immediate, intense, and clear. Nothing of what he said or wrote felt even remotely familiar to me. Nothing came through me; it all came through him as he just happened to be sitting in my energy field! It was a little trippy when I felt him come in. I could hear him say, "I am a famous writer." I felt like a man and felt myself get fatter—no disrespect intended. And I— me in my own mind and thinking—was excited to see who it was and scared about the bar that was being set all at the same time. I just went with it, asked no questions, went deeper if I felt myself becoming too present, and stayed out of his way. I listened to his thoughts and kept my eyes on the keypad. He stopped—literally stopped my hands—if

I was about to write something that did not come from him. It almost felt like I couldn't command my body because he was commanding it and had access to my limbs at that moment. When he finished and disengaged from my energy, I could feel his presence still there in the room with me, and I wanted to ask him some questions and dialogue with him. He quickly left, and the room was empty, except for me. Such a larger than life presence—unmistakable to anyone, even those who do not have sensitivity to such things. I could hear him laughing as he left. I heard it inside my head just like with regular mental mediumship. It got more distant as his energy dissipated and disconnected. I was now fully returned to myself. I had no idea what he wrote until I went back and read it. His perspective on his work was interesting, and I feel it can only be verified by those closest to him. I found it extremely touching that what he wanted to convey—what I feel was most important to him in this connection—was to speak with his loved ones and to make right some wrongs. This famous man—infamous, really—was just like everyone else. He wanted to speak with his loved ones and apologize. He did not ask me to give them the messages or hope that they got it through the writing; he spoke directly to them—he spoke through me and at times, to me. I believe the *Re* he is referring to was a woman he had known who was the muse for his character Renata. This man gave very clear evidence that only those closest to him would recognize. We have all been given the gift to glimpse beyond the fame and persona of this man and witness his authenticity and his heart. This story illustrates how important relationships are to all of us, no matter who we are or what kind of lives we've lived. It also illustrates how death often provides the opportunity for us to make amends and seek forgiveness so that healing can begin. Thank you, Ernest, for a life-changing experience.

—Ro, written May 17, 2012

11
BLANCHE

Sometimes It Takes a Lifetime

I am already in the power, waiting anxiously for a spirit to come and speak to me. I can feel the excitement of those in spirit as they wait to connect to me and tell their stories. It feels like the word has gotten out in heaven, letting all know that I am here to take dictation—to bring their stories and experiences to this world. I am ready to serve any way I can....

I am in the presence of a woman, and while I am psychically connecting to her, I can sense she is very, very beautiful and very regal. She has a starlet quality to her, and I see her silhouette in my mind's eye. The picture I see is black and white, but I can tell she has very dark, luminous, soulful eyes. She speaks to me....

*

My name is Blanche and I was born in 1912. My family was well off in the standards of those days. I grew up just outside of Philadelphia in a suburb called Roxy. My father was a businessman in the city and my mother was, well, a mother. My parents had met through a mutual acquaintance and married within six months of meeting. My mother recognized a good prospect when she saw one and figured he was as good a chance as any to make the kind of life she wanted to live. They were both from families with means, and she was never going to marry below her family's financial status. She never thought of marriage as a love endeavor—more an arrangement that affords one a lifestyle. My father, on the other hand, adored my mother and was hell bent on making her his wife from the moment he saw her. He was also a man that acquired possessions, and he felt she was a nice trophy to add to his collection of refined things. He was a bit older than her and already established when they met, and her innocence and style appealed to him. The fact that she could care less for him was also a big intrigue and made him want her even more. I was born ten months after their marriage. My mother had a rough time in delivery and almost died. It took her months to recover, and I was taken care of by my aunt Susanne—my mother's younger sister—and by a wet nurse named Clara. I was named for a Philadelphia opera singer, Blanche Cavanaugh, whom my parents shared a common passion for. My mother, already aloof and emotionally detached by nature, had a very hard time connecting with me. Add to that her near death and trauma from my birth and the fact that she was only nineteen and ill-equipped to care for herself let alone an infant and you have the makings for a disastrous mother-daughter bonding experience. My father hired help, of course, but my mother would be so curt and sometimes harassing to them, they would leave. My aunt Susanne would come to help, but my mother resented the closeness she felt for me. Her lack of nurturing abilities became more obvious when my aunt was around, so visits were not encouraged or welcomed. By the time I was three, I regarded my mother as a distant acquaintance. She kept my father at arm's length too, fearing another pregnancy, which she felt she could not bear and definitely did not want. I viewed my mother with curiosity and nothing more and was polite in her presence but felt no real love or connection to her. My father was not home often, conducting business and seeking comfort and understanding in other women, but when he was he was warm, loving, and affectionate—all the things my mother was not. When it was time for me to go to school, the nanny had arranged for me to go to a private school in North Philadelphia. She also arranged for piano lessons and singing lessons at that time, as I was showing an ability to sing. My mother left all details of my care and upbringing to this wonderful nanny, Helene, and my father gladly paid for anything and everything that she suggested. I was his only child, and he was determined to offer me the world—as long as someone else arranged it. My mother resented Helene's connection to me, and Helene was smart enough to hide her devotion and love for me in front of my mother. It seems while my mother could not be close to me—or anyone else—she did not want anyone else to be close to me either. She resented that others could and wanted to give me what she could not. Helene knew she walked a fine line with my mother, and she figured out ways to lessen the obvious love and sense of responsibility she felt for me, so as not challenge my mother and possibly cause us to be separated. By the time I was nine years old, my aunt Susanne was taking me to operas and theater. I was fascinated. My father would provide the means and, of course, would deny me nothing. By this time, my mother had finally recovered from my birth and was busy with her own life again of socializing, partying, and shopping. She had no real friends though. She rarely spent time with my father, only showing up when it was for appearances and business. I think, even until the day he died, he always hoped she would one day at least pay attention to him, or want to be with him. It never happened, and it never happened for me either. At twelve I was sent to boarding school in Connecticut. I was used to the cold, unemotional environment, having grown up in a household like that. Still, I missed home, my things, and most of all, I missed Helene. We had to hold back our tears for fear of any retribution from my mother if she witnessed any tenderness between us. Helene was let go after I left, and I didn't know this until I returned home for the winter holidays. I had to cry in my room so my mother wouldn't see. I had to act like it did not affect me at all when I was in the presence of anyone (except my father), as everyone was instructed to report to my mother about my behavior. I asked my aunt Susanne to find out where Helene was so I could write her a letter. She hesitated and it took a while, but with my persistence, she finally acquiesced, and I was able to send Helene a note. I knew she would never take the chance to send one back to me, but somehow I was sure she had received it and read it.

I would send Helene notes for the next ten years, again, never receiving confirmation but always sure she was reading them. I would tell her about school and what I was learning and experiencing. I would share all my deepest thoughts and secrets. I would always tell her I loved her and missed her—words I never said to anyone else, not even my dad. In my senior year of high school, there was some sort of world financial crisis, and my father lost a major amount of money. So did his family, and even some of my mother's family. While it had been expected that I would go to college, here was the perfect opportunity for me to change that plan. I decided to go to New York City and try my hand in theater. My father was too distracted with financial ruin to object, and my mother, as usual, could care less. I did have some of my own savings, accumulated through gifts and some inheritance from my maternal grandfather. I got an apartment on the West Side and looked immediately for a singing and acting coach. I had been studying voice since I was child and played the piano and flute with great proficiency, but I had never studied acting. In school I had been part of all the plays and productions, but mostly for singing and as an accompanist on the piano. New York was much different than Philly, and certainly a new world compared to Connecticut. I loved it and felt so free and so relaxed. I would document everything to Helene in letters. Soon I got a part in a small play produced by a man named Weinberg. He was the first Jewish man I had ever met. I was meeting so many different cultures, religions, and foods in this wonderful city. I quickly realized too that not everyone had money and that there were many people who struggled to exist; I had never seen that before. I was auditioning for more roles and getting them. The fact that I was an accomplished singer afforded me many opportunities and opened many doors for me. No one knew my family, no one knew my background, and frankly, no one cared. I was accepted and honored for my own merits and accomplishments. I began to gather quite a bit of theater experience under my belt. My father had somewhat financially recovered by the time I was twenty-five and was able to visit and see some of my work. My mother would come with him, looking for any opportunity to visit New York City, but she would not come to my shows or to see me perform. She usually got a headache or was too tired from shopping. She would manage to join us for a late supper after, only because she would be hungry. My father was very proud of me and my accomplishments—surprising for a man of his generation—and never pressured me to get married or leave this life I was building and creating. I became a quite successful Broadway artist; my talent as an actress was as strong as my singing. I starred in many productions. My favorites were *Bye Bye Birdie* and *Guinevere*. By the forties, I had established my own financial success in theater and had moved to the Upper East Side of Manhattan. My life afforded me opportunities to meet many men, and I had many suitors—lovers, really—who were always more interested in me than I was in them. My love and affection was always the theater, and it took up most of my time and attention. I had stopped writing to Helene in my early twenties when things got busy, but I never stopped thinking of her, and she never left my heart. One day, after my performance in *The Unsinkable Molly Brown*, a stage assistant knocked on my door and announced there was someone here to see me. It was Helene and her daughter, Mary. I have never felt such rush of emotions in my life; it was if my heart burst wide open in seeing Helene standing there, and it was as if no time had passed between us. We hugged for a very long time; I did not want to let her go. Mary looked on with such happiness and joy at our reunion, and I thought about how my mother would react if she was here to witness this. We sat and talked for a long time, and Helene pulled out the stack of notes I had sent her, wrapped in a pink ribbon. She had kept every letter, and reread them often. She loved me, and I loved her, and in that moment it was okay to know this and act this way—how freeing that was. I took them to meet the cast, and then we had dinner in a small café near my apartment. I wanted them to stay with me, but they had a room at the Belmont Hotel and would be leaving for Pennsylvania in the morning. Three months after that meeting Helene died of what was believed to be an aneurism. I returned to Philly for her funeral. I took the opportunity to visit my parents' home—I hadn't been back there since I left at eighteen. It was exactly the same, kept the same, and felt the same—cold, empty, lonely, expensive. My father was home, having semi-retired due to poor health. My mother had not retired from her shopping and socializing. I sat with my father expressing to him my sorrow over Helene. I confided that I had written to her for years and that she had kept and cherished those letters. I spoke of how heartbroken I was when she was let go and of how thrilled I was when I got to see her again, three months ago. My mother must have returned, and in passing the study on the way to her bedroom, had overheard my conversation with my father. She entered and stared at me with a mix of distance, disdain, and disgust. She then laughed and said how ridiculous I sounded talking about Helene. In that moment, the politeness I always showed this woman vanished. I told her Helene was the mother I never had and I was grateful, very grateful, to have had her in my life. I told her I felt sorry for the cold, bitter, nasty woman she was and always had been, but the one good thing she ever did for me was allow Helene to *love* me. I said a word my mother did not know and could not even comprehend. I deliberately lashed out because I was hurting, and in that moment I wanted to hurt this woman too. There was complete silence. My father did not interfere. I think he was relieved I had finally said this to her. I got up and left and didn't speak to her for years…not even when I returned home for my father's funeral.

I lost the woman that brought me into this world and my real mother on that day. Like my biological mother, I took my emotions and locked them away, getting on with my life, moving forward with the path I had chosen. In 1956, my aunt Susanne called to tell me my mother was sick and that things were not looking good. She told me she thought I should know but completely understood if I did not want to come and visit. There was no pressure; she was just giving me the information. At first I dismissed the conversation. I had long ago buried this woman, so at first it did not seem to faze me. About a week after that phone call, I felt compelled to visit my mother. The house was exactly as it had always been. It had been refurbished many times but never updated or changed. My mother was in her bedroom, and there was a full-time private nurse with her. She struggled to breathe as I entered the room. I sat by her bed—her usual indifference was still intact and unwavering. I didn't speak or touch her, just sat and stared. This went on for days. She could care less if I was there or not—I knew—yet I felt completely compelled to stay there. I would watch the help tend to her…she treated us all equally. One morning when I was sitting by the window alternating looking at her and looking at the man cutting the grass, I realized, like an epiphany, she has never been capable of anything more. She did not know how to make a connection to someone, anyone, or anything. It was like a gong had gone off in my head. She could not give what she did not have to give, and she could not give what she did not know. I don't know why this was, nor did I care; I just knew what it was. In that moment my mother looked at me, we locked eyes, and for the first time in my entire life—and I am sure in hers—I felt connected to her. A moment later she took her last breath.

I didn't understand why I was returning to see her—certainly I was never expecting that. I had cut her off that day after Helene's funeral. I was very capable of that, after all; I had her genes. I had never longed for my mother's love as child or wondered if there was something wrong with me because she could not love me. Somewhere I must have known this truth about her, but in that moment of clarity it completely set both of us free. My heart was very light after that, and I finally felt loving and connected to my mother. I have since learned that in that moment, she was set free also. She was freed of whatever restraints or whatever reasons she had for being, in current language, emotionally unavailable. I am assured; future life experiences will not have that same component.

I died of lung cancer in 1972 having had a successful theater career and wonderful and fulfilling life. I regret nothing, nor would I change or wish for anything to have been different. As I passed from physical to spirit, my mother was there to greet me...along with Helene, my father, and many good friends I had made in my lifetime as Blanche. I was told I had lived a very rewarding, emotional life by them all.

With love,

Blanche

*

Blanche shows us that one moment of love can wipe away a lifetime of emptiness. In the end, Blanche and her mother realized that they were always connected and that the energy of love could be felt and understood. This allowed them to transcend any and all pain and their hurt. In one instant, through the connection Blanche and her mother made with their eyes, a lifetime of disconnect ended, and love healed the rift between them. How lucky for them that they seized the opportunity that presented itself.

We have the choice to make any kind of life we want. We either create fate or destiny. When we allow our fear, our hurt, our ego to react or choose, we create fate, like Blanche's mother. When we come from our soul (spirit), we live our destiny. While Blanche's mother fated their relationship with her choices, the destiny of their souls was fulfilled in those last moments of her life. Blanche did not let her mother's choices hold her back though. She did not use her own life experiences to make excuses for what she could or could not do or be. She did not allow her ego or wounds to dictate her choice in that moment either. She allowed her heart to remain open and receive her mother's love when it became available. Her example shows us that we can choose to let nothing hold us back. That one moment in their lifetime changed the course of their destiny, released the karma, and healed their past.

We will all receive such graces in our lives as well. Divinity will always offer interventions, moments of clarity, unexpected assistance, and support. We just have to be ready. We just have to come from our spirit, and the rest will take care of itself.

—Ro, written September 25, 2012

SECTION THREE

STORIES OF
LESSONS IN DEATH

12
REBECCA'S STORY

This was the very first story I wrote. I set some time aside one morning and sat to meditate for a bit to clear my mind and "power up." I had no idea what to expect, what would come (if anything would come), or what I was doing. I only knew that I was to sit and let those from spirit come to me. I sat and sort of waited until I felt compelled to write. My grandfather and father, who are in spirit, and Ben Franklin, who often shows up as a spirit guide for me, were all present. Suddenly, I felt comfortable, ready, and open. I became aware of a young woman speaking to me in my consciousness. At one point, she sat in the room with me, and her presence was very noticeable. I could hear her more than I could see her. As she described her situation, I felt as if I were taking dictation. After I finished writing her words, I read the story. I really absorbed what she was saying. I could feel all of her emotions and those of her parents. I could feel her compassion for them, and then eventually for herself and her situation. I realized that this was more than a story—it was an inspirational message, and it carried an energy vibration that was affecting me, changing me. I had no idea at this point why I was connecting to this woman or if I was to share her information with anyone. I had no idea if anyone would find this interesting or worth reading or if they would feel the energy of it the same way I had. What amazed me most was that as I reread the story, I realized there were no typing errors and that it seemed to need no correction or editing. A few days later I reread it again. If I went to change anything, I was guided not to; it was complete as it was. I was intrigued by the last sentence and the geographical location it referred to. Not knowing if there was a Warren County, Ohio, I Googled it and was shocked to discover it existed. I then Googled 1986 and checked obituaries for that time for anyone named Rebecca, age twenty-eight. As I was about to push enter, I heard, felt, and sensed very clearly I was not to go any further—that somehow this would taint or influence what I was doing or how I was supposed to do it. Spirit told me these things could be verified but not by me. Any further attempts made with other stories turned out the same way. I was not supposed to seek this information. So I learned and trusted that when I receive information that does not come from any frame of reference within me, I can simply ask spirit for confirmation to put my mind at ease, and I always get it in one form or another.

I somehow felt different after writing this story. For the next three weeks, I sat on the same day, at the same time, and wrote for whoever came in. Same process, same reread with the same results, but every story, every dictation, completely different. Even the process and the way I received the information changed with each writing. On the days I would write, my whole house felt different. Everyone who lived here noticed this. It was after the fifth story that I realized spirit was making a compilation of stories and that each was going to be unique. Still, I did not know if these stories were book-worthy or if anyone would care or be affected by them the same way I was. Week after week, I just kept showing up and allowing whatever needed to be told to come through.

Rebecca's story is my favorite story in this compilation, maybe because she was the first to come to me, but also because she taught me so much about just letting go and letting my consciousness expand. I felt then and still feel limitless because of her. I am forever grateful.

*

My father and grandfather immediately step in—there is such an overwhelming excitement as they have been waiting for me to enter this space. Ben Franklin is here too, not sitting on the couch peering over his glasses, instead standing in the doorway waiting for me to acknowledge him. "We may begin now," are his words. They are patient and slow.

Ben brings a lady in. She is shy and sits on the sofa. Dad is to my left and Grandpa Roger is behind me....

Rebecca speaks:

My name is Rebecca. They told me I could come and speak to you—that you could and would listen. I come from a devoutly religious family that would never believe in such things. Shunned and exiled is how my existence would have been if I even spoke of such things while alive. It was the summer of my twenty-eighth year on earth when I passed. My car hydroplaned on the slick nighttime road. My father's Oldsmobile went over the guard rail and into cool, dark water below the bridge. I stood on the bridge waiting for someone to discover my body...to discover what happened to me. It took over a week before they found the car and me....They never found out what happened—until now.

When I drowned, I thought I was still alive. I came out of the water, crawled up the river bank, and made it to the bridge. I found it odd at first that no one noticed me and that nothing seemed to hurt in my body. Cars would pass and I would waive them down. Soon, a police car passed, and I jumped in front of it. He did not see me, and his patrol car passed right through me, effortlessly. In that moment, I knew I was no longer alive as I had known life to be. I waited and waited. As I began to worry about my parents and what they must be thinking I suddenly found I was with them. Exuberant, I would try and get their attention, but they could not hear or see me. Devastated, I resorted to being present without their knowledge or sense of that. I was sitting in the silent living room when the police knocked on the door. My dad was reading the newspaper. The headlines that day spoke of the inflation rate and cutting taxes. He assumed I disappeared of my own accord, and his anger was all he could feel—not the love or compassion I brought to the room. My mom, in her blue plaid dress with the apron I had sewn for her, was in the kitchen trying to keep busy. She wiped her hands in her apron as the doorbell rang, and for a moment, she briefly felt my presence. Her intuition had already told her who was at the door and what she was about to hear. My dad had no clue. His anger intensified after he learned of my death. His mind found many reasons to feel anger.

Once, I found myself thinking of California, and suddenly I was transported there. I panicked, not knowing how I got there or how I would get back. Then I remembered and thought of the bridge…. Instantaneously, I was there. I realized that I moved with thought—it was a complete shift in my consciousness.

After my body was found, I had to consciously choose where I would be. As I thought of someone or someplace, I would be there. It took a while but I began to get the knack of this and use it with great advantage. I was desperate to tell my family what happened, especially my dad. He wondered all the rest of his life if I had committed suicide. I longed to ease his pain. He would have understood that as an animal lover—really a lover of the sacredness of all living forms—I would have done anything to avoid hitting the animal in the road. My physical death was unintentional, and knowing that could have changed his perception. It would have given him the opportunity to open his heart again. Once I tried to come in his dream state. He interpreted it as a nightmare and woke up startled and upset, never speaking about it, not even to my mother. My mom would allow me into her dreams. We would embrace and connect, and then her sadness would sever the link and she would experience me fading away.

She would grasp for me but could not hold on. She would wake up sad the next day, and I longed to comfort her. I remembered how to send my love to her through thought and intention. She would feel the warmth and comfort, but she never knew, never realized that's what it was. I could be satisfied with that.

Like me, it took my dad a while to release his earth mind when he passed. I caught on to the fact that I could "travel" anywhere about three month's post physical death. That realization allowed me to then transcend. I immediately met the faces that represented my ancestors. Even though I never met them while on earth, I knew them. They helped me to understand the process of *soul return*, as they called it. And they helped my father—when he was ready. My mother had no problem passing. She was eager and ready, looking forward to seeing me and my father again. Her only adjustment was to the change from what her religious beliefs held and what she experienced. She was a strict and devout Mormon, as was my father. Their "view-perception" of what happened after physical death differed greatly from what they experienced. There was a brief moment where my father experienced "judgment." In the process of physical death, there is a moment of release of fear consciousness. It is like earth's gravity has been released and you are free floating. In that split second, your soul remembrance has a chance to enter your thoughts, and when it does, you are free of the limits that have often held you back, separated you, or defined you while on earth. That moment is a divine gift given to every soul. It allowed my father freedom to experience love.

My name is Rebecca. I lived in 1958, died in 1986. My parents were Marshall and Elinore. My sister, Jean, passed in 1994. Her daughter, Rose Ellen, still lives in Warren County, Ohio.

*

I have found through countess medium readings that it is important for those in spirit who have passed to tell their story. This is especially true for those who have passed under mysterious circumstances, including suicide. It is important to let others know what happened.

This is, of course, to help those still living find peace, but also so the events can be witnessed and acknowledged. It helps release any emotional trauma held by the spirit and those who are living, so that healing may occur. Telling our story helps to heal it, whether we are alive or dead.

I feel Rebecca moved into greater peace after revealing her story. And I hope Rebecca's dad finds the understanding and compassion that he could not when he was on earth. I wish he could have changed his thinking. I wish he could have opened his heart more to his daughter when she was alive as well as after she passed. His experience and his life could have been so different.

Maybe Rose Ellen will read her aunt's story, and maybe they will finally understand Rebecca's last moments on earth.

—Ro, written October 5, 2010

13
MANDY

Finding Purpose Through Death

By the time I sat to write Mandy's story, I had developed a rhythm with this process and a ritual to set the tone. I would light a candle and sit quietly to meditate. After grounding myself and opening the space for whoever wanted to visit, I would allow my now still mind to receive images, impressions, thoughts, or words from those connecting from spirit. On this day, I was aware of an older woman coming through to me. As she began speaking to me, her energy felt much younger and more vital than what I was perceiving. Afterwards I realized I was getting the image of her on earth—as the old woman— but the energy was matching the vitality and vibrance she attained through her evolution in death. This was very interesting and revealing to me. I was experiencing her as she was on earth and as she is now in spirit. This taught me that the cycles and rhythms we experience on earth continue and that while our physical bodies get old and wither, our spirit energy can and often does reveal a different story. This was a new concept for me, and I had not previously experienced this through my mediumistic abilities. I did experience this phenomenon more frequently in private and platform readings after this writing. It has taught me a great deal about the dimensions of our physical and spiritual energy, as well as our mental and emotional energy. Mandy's story is truly inspiring for all of us, showing that growth and new beginnings can happen at any time—even post death.

*

My name is Mandy. I come from Australia, or at least I did when I was alive. I moved to the US when I was fifteen years old. Returned to Australia in my twenties to go to university, and then came back to the US when I was thirty. I married a man named Frank Cassella—a New York City man; his family was from Poughkeepsie. We had three beautiful children together: Hannah, Samantha, and Steven. They were my joy in life. Our marriage was very rocky at times. My husband could be very secretive, and I didn't ask too many questions. Part of me was afraid of the answers. All and all I had a good life—nothing extraordinary, but a good life. I was not always happy or fulfilled, but nothing really devastating happened, and compared to what others experience in life, I felt lucky. I died at the age of seventy years old—well, seventy and a few months actually. I had kidney failure due to complications from diabetes. Funny, my diabetes was never out of control, but it did take a toll on my kidneys, and then I was done. My family was with me in the hospital when I passed. They knew and accepted it was coming. There was nothing remarkable about my passing; I simply slipped out of my body—what looks like into a coma—and then I left with the help of a beautiful angel who appeared as I passed. She helped me leave this life and move on. I was neither religious nor spiritual in life. I was raised Presbyterian but followed this religion more of habit than of faith. I did not give much thought to the meaning of life or its purpose. I did not give much thought to my purpose—instead just going with what came next for me. I did not worry much in life either, as I had no expectations. Some would say this was a very good thing.

My children were (are) more thoughtful on such matters. They each developed a level of spirituality that I could not identify with. To each his own, I guess. I came to speak with you as I wanted to share how things have unfolded for me since I passed in 1981.... I know—a long time ago.

When I first returned to "home" I was confused a bit—again, never giving much thought to the afterlife or what is referred to as God. I simply continued with my life-mind pattern of just going with whatever. I was brought to a place where I immediately connected to my previous earth family—a reunion of sorts. All of the people in my life were there, even the ones I had not met in life.... Grandparents, great grandparents, cousins, aunts, uncles, and so, so many more.... It was overwhelming in scope, but the love that surrounded me was what really changed things. I felt washed and cleansed by the intense love, devotion, and compassion that was emanating towards me from all of these people. Soon I began to emerge and remember who I was. Any and all illusions of that previous earth life were melted away. I felt clear and whole—healed, if you will. I began to feel the depth of love and joy that had always been within me—always had been me. I realized how I had gone through life mostly unaware of the brilliance within me and the brilliance I was. It was not that I had strayed from myself or lost myself—more as if I had not fully been myself. I now understood what my children had known—were aware of in life.

Soon I found myself enjoying what feels like the pleasures of earth within this new realm. I did not miss my family, because I never felt separated from them. I did feel creative and ready to extend myself forward and begin new things—start a new life. At first I delved into the things I enjoyed while on earth: reading, sewing, crocheting, baking. I delighted in these things like I hadn't on earth. Everything was a magnificent, unique creation, and I was inspired for more after each one. I then began to explore other talents and possibilities within me. I began to cultivate a garden and learn ways to enhance the life force within the vegetables I grew. I could feel the connection to my children's and grandchildren's minds. As I worked on this from my realm, they learned this in their realm—earth—and brought into physical manifestation there. When I worked on sustainable energy through gardening, they received the thought as well and implemented it into their lives. One of my grandsons, Mark, is studying environmental science and will bring forth many new and innovative technologies for good earth living as I develop and work with them in my realm. And I am not just doing it; my family, my line, the soul connection from this realm is also working on this. We were a line of farmers on earth, and even though I did not follow that path in that life, it was still part of my soul "genetics" and is coming through now. My purpose is powerful and clear. What I am doing from spirit directly affects my earth family and also the global family of earth. Purpose can always be found and fulfilled. Life does not stop or cease, and everything is tied together…and all actions affect everything and everyone. I am more connected to life now than I was on earth, and my family—my children—can feel this and understand this. It comforts them. For me, life is great. This is what is referred to as bliss. I have found my bliss.

I am happy you received me today. I am happy to share with you my story. My name is Mandy. We have been speaking of the Peirce family connection. With peace to you.

*

Through Mandy's death we learn that we are always growing and evolving. Our consciousness shifts, and it is through the power of love that this becomes possible. Even death itself offers new opportunities both for experiences and expansion of our awareness. Mandy's story illustrates that life continues after death and that we always remain connected to our loved ones through love, thought, and energy. We can contribute to earth life from spirit and help create new pathways for better living. Mandy found hidden pieces of herself after her death and cultivated them and then shared them with her living earth family. Maybe if we pay attention we will realize our loved ones are working and helping us too.

—Ro, written February 16, 2011

14
CONNIE

A Message of Love for My Children

The morning I sat to write Connie's message, I was aware of the presence of Archangel Gabriel. This archangel is the messenger angel—she assists all forms of communication, especially telepathic, prophetic, and inspirational communication. She governs the sense of clairaudience. Her presence and power was helping, inspiring, and connecting to me all morning. On this specific day, she was instrumental in carving out some time and space for me to write. As I sat to receive my yet unknown spirit visitor, I became aware of an extreme emotional energy. It was a combination anxiety, eagerness, excitement, impatience, and sadness. Emotional energy is very different than spiritual energy. It is magnetic in feel and can be very dense and intense. Emotions are an earthly experience. Our spirit does not hold emotions and does not have emotional reactions to earth (or other) experiences.

Spirit energy is like the radiance of the sun, whereas emotional energy feels like the clouds that block or pass the sun. When we are in spirit, we lose the emotional component of our being and return to pure energy—love. When a medium senses emotional energy connected to a spirit presence, it is a residual energy charge left behind (like a lingering perfume), and can often reveal the state of consciousness of the spirit just before death, or even the emotional makeup of that person in their lifetime. It is evidential information about the person coming through. The consciousness we become after death will sometimes connect to the earthly emotions to punctuate a message or to carry the energy into the physical realm or to or through the medium. This is what I was feeling or sensing for this particular writing session. Afterwards, I realized this message was sent on the emotional energy of a mother's deep love for her children, and some of the other feelings were more resonant with my own—my own reaction to a message I hadn't gotten yet but would soon have.

*

My name is Connie. I come from Milwaukee. I have waited so long to connect to someone. Your mom and dad told me you would help me—that you could find my children for me and let them know I am okay; I am here.

I was in a car accident. It was very icy out. I left the kids home and went to get milk and bread. I left on a bad note. They were home all day from school—a snow day—and were driving me crazy. I told them I was going out and not coming home, and then I didn't. I didn't mean this, of course; I was speaking from my frustration and annoyance. Then it happened, and I haven't been able to let them know I didn't mean this. I have three of the most beautiful children you could ever imagine. My oldest, Steven, was fifteen when I passed. He is very mature—more than most boys his age. He had to be. I was a single mom, and he assumed the role of assistant adult for me. He helped keep the other two in line. It was hard when their dad and I separated. Steven was only ten. His dad left town shortly after for a new job in Michigan. They only see him in the summer. While their father loves them, distance had strained the relationships he has with the children. My middle child is Britney. She was almost fourteen when I passed—just beginning to get that teenage angst and mother-daughter conflict setting in. We were always close. She's my only girl, but as she hit teens, and the tension of divorce, we had our rifts. Nothing irreparable—certainly all forgotten by me as quickly as they happened. My youngest is Derek. He was only ten when I passed. Being the youngest, his brother and sister always try and protect him—yet he has a great innate wisdom that allows him to understand things most people cannot. It was a Wednesday. I left at 6:45. Had to get out of the house. I was so worried that I would not have stuff for breakfast and lunch the next day. I was annoyed; they had been home all day due to the snow. We had been stuck in quite often with bad weather—everyone had a bit of cabin fever. When I left I was yelling, telling them I would be back whenever or maybe I wouldn't come back at all. I immediately regretted this. Sitting in the car I kept thinking, *What a horrible thing to say to your kids, especially since they have a dad who left and they rarely see.* I would tell them I was sorry as soon as I got home. As I was pulling out of the driveway, Derek ran to the car to give me my gloves. He startled me. I rolled down the window, and without a word he handed them to me. His look was so intent though not emotional—just like he was taking in all he could, looking at me so he would imprint my image clearly in his mind. I didn't realize it was the last time he would see me. My opportunity to apologize came—and went. All I said was, "Thanks," then, "Love you," and I pulled out. He stood and watched me, and for a moment, my insides told me to pull back in and go inside. My mind overruled that with its own intent, and I drove off towards town. I got to the grocery store—FoodMart—about 7:10. Roads were very slippery, and not many people were driving. I got the damn milk and eggs and some ice cream—rocky road and cookie dough. A peace offering for my kids...thought it would go nice with the apology. I walked back to the car, almost falling twice in the parking lot. No thoughts entered my mind that my physical death was imminent. People wonder if you know you are going to die. From my experience, no—I had no clue that this was it. No intuition, no warning, nothing. I started my car and it did not immediately turn over. This was a newer car—never had a problem. My thought was, *Is it really that cold? Could this happen so quickly?* For a brief moment I thought of going back into the store and calling the kids to let them know I was stuck. Had I done that, I would still be alive. As I found in hindsight, timing is everything. I kept trying until the car turned over—took only the third try. As soon as it started, I sped away, not even waiting for it to warm up. For someone who was in such a rush to get out of the house, I was in even more of a rush to get home.

I never saw the truck coming. Just as I pulled out of the parking lot, in my own race to get home and only looking in one direction, a large white box truck hit me broadside. The groceries on the front seat sprayed through the windshield. I barely felt the impact to my right. My last thought was that they would not get the ice cream…. Then I saw Derek's face—and it was my chance to imprint his image completely in my mind. When the police rang the bell a little after 10:00 p.m. that evening, Derek was the one to answer the door. He knew without them telling him. My neighbor Jessica allowed the kids to stay with her that evening. I could do nothing to help them, but I was allowed to observe them at this time. I was amazed how everything was orchestrated from this realm I now found myself in. The energy of love and compassion flooded around them. From earth and human perspective, one does not even know this is happening, let alone "sees" it. But from the realm of spirit, it is like sound waves rolling in and around everyone involved. As soon as Jessica answered the door for the officers, she was engulfed in it too—and then, as if it awakened within her, she began exuding this energy as well. When the kids called George, their dad, it surrounded him and extended from him as well. I stood off the earth at this time—stood with my dad, Howard, and watched as it all played out…as my experience, my life and death, impacted theirs. I watched as spirit took over and unleashed all the love that is in the universe into this situation, into these people. I wondered, *Is it always like this?* and as soon as I did, I knew, heard, and felt the answer: *Yes.* It is always there, and the death experience awakens the potential for the full force of love and compassion to become present.

My kids went to live with their dad after that. I am happy to say they are thriving, and their lives are going on very well. Still, my death impacted them deeply and created a detour, if you will, in their direction. I didn't have to die that day. Had I paid more attention to my intuition—had I known how—I probably wouldn't have left the house that night. My will fueled my actions, not my inner guidance. Still, spirit does damage control, and my children did not suffer for my choices. Their life, while turned upside down, was made right by their choices, the support of spirit, and the energy of love, which they readily accepted and did not resist or push away. I want them to know I love them. I did not mean what I said, and I am so sorry I hurt them with my words. I want them to know they were the best children a mother could ever have and that I am so proud of them and who they have become in this world. Let them know I am always here for them, that our hearts and energies are still connected, that I watch over them and see their lives unfold. Please, call on me, in your heart and mind, out loud or silently, and I will hear you and be there. I am your mother in this life, and I will always be with you.

—Connie S.

*

We all have intuition—that gut feeling or inner knowing. It is subtle, not loud. It does not speak in your head, instead coming as a feeling, usually of unease. Whenever we get that feeling it is our opportunity to get still and go inside and listen. Most of us rarely do that, and most of our intuitive information goes unnoticed and unheard. When we do pay attention, we increase our spiritual awareness and develop a greater intimacy with our true *self* and with divinity. Connie was receiving intuitive hits, but her focus was outward and not inward. She dismissed her inner knowing. And it seems spirit really tried to intervene and spare Connie this fate, but her free will kept interfering. Sometimes our minds are more forceful than spirit. When that happens we create a fate instead of living our destiny. I wish Connie had listened to that subtle voice telling her to stay home. I hope Connie's children read this story and can find peace in knowing that she loves them and is sorry for her words. Connie's gift to all of us is to remember the power and impact of our words and to be mindful of the things we say from emotion. She is letting us know the power of a mother's love that makes her determined to make things right with her children. My wish is that her story helps them.

—Ro, written February 2, 2011

15
LISA ANN

The Power of Acceptance

I was eager to see what and who would come through today. I felt calmer than usual, and as the story unfolded I realized why. As I wrote Lisa Ann's words, I could feel her strength, courage, and conviction; I could feel her peace. Like other stories and readings, I was connecting to Lisa Ann through my own emotional energy field first.

Clearly, writing these stories was affecting me in a very positive way. I wondered how her experience and vibration influenced or had affected her family and if the peace she radiates extended to them like it did (and still does) to me. After reading her story, I also wondered if I will be able to handle my own death when the time comes, the same way Lisa Ann did. I hope so, and I also hope she will be there to meet me.

*

My name is Lisa—Lisa Ann. I died three years ago at the age of twenty-seven from terminal cancer. It started as a sore on my right ankle—turned out it was not just an average sore; it was a sarcoma, and it had invaded the bone. I went through very aggressive treatments—conventional and unconventional. I traveled to Mexico and saw a man who gave me coffee enemas and extreme intravenous vitamin therapy. It did not help. Finally, I went to a faith healer in Arizona. He was a very wise and gentle man with Native American roots. He told me that my healing would come by accepting and embracing my impending physical death, not by fighting against what I knew to be true. At first, I wanted to rage at him—*How dare you! I am only twenty-seven years old. I haven't even begun to live.* But a part of me not only *knew* this was the truth but was relieved to hear someone say it out loud. It was like I was suddenly free and let out of a cage. I soon packed my bags and left Arizona, returning to my home where my parents waited anxiously for my return and news. I sat with them and told them it was now time for me to prepare to die—that my death was not imminent, but at best, we had a few months. This was late August; I had been diagnosed twenty-six months prior. I should say my life turned into a living hell twenty-six month before—but now, I could feel the return of peace; I could feel my changing once again, only this time for the better.

To say my parents were shocked is an understatement. They lamented over and over how there could be more treatments, more options. They had never agreed with the faith healing thing but would have tried anything if there was even a remote option it would save me. They were desperate. I understood that, but I also knew what I heard from that man was the truth, and the truth was my path to freedom and peace. I can't say I accepted it immediately either or that I didn't have my moments even after I accepted it. I wanted to live…I wanted all the things everyone else wants: meaningful work, a husband, family, home. I had to mourn all the experiences I did not think I was going to get; yet, there was a peace about this and about me at the same time. Somewhere, I knew, I may not get these things now or in this concept of now, but I would get them and have an even deeper appreciation for them. My mind would process this one way but my heart and core processed it another. Funny, I had not been very spiritual or religious up until this time, but after that meeting, it was like a vault of "knowing" inside of me opened, and I could access this deep wisdom and peace.

Eventually my family and fiancé began to come around. There was a lot of crying in the beginning, and some were even mad at me for "giving up," but I believe there was a divine grace working with everyone at that time, bringing them to the place where they could come into their heart of love and out of their heart of pain and sorrow.

As soon as I accepted this, it was as if my body breathed a sigh of relief. I actually felt stronger and healthier than I had in twenty-six months. The pain I had been experiencing all through my body subsided. I hardly needed pain meds. Once I stopped chemo and even some vitamins, herbs, and concoctions, I was no longer nauseous or fatigued. Miraculously, my insurance company who had been giving me all kinds of trouble began to pay old claims with no problem. I was on disability and was subsidizing this with savings. When I realized I didn't need savings, it seemed that my expenses reduced and there was more money everywhere! Then I realized, I had a 401(k) with my job—a job I was clinging to because I thought once I was past this I would need it to get on with living and to pay back all my medical expenses. Realizing I didn't need to save this for retirement any longer, I took this money out (against the sound advice of my accountant— you know, just in case) and felt like all bets were off. I took my family to Disney for two weeks. My mom, realizing that she had no choice but to honor my beliefs and wishes, decided that if she only had a few months with me, then she was going to spend every moment of that with me, and she quit her teaching job of twenty-four years—retired, really. My dad didn't really have that luxury; after all, they were going to continue to live after I was gone, and someone had to hold the line, but he did take extended time off, used all his sick days and vacation time, and then, in the end, he even took some family leave. What a glorious time we had in those months.

I would wake up about ten in the morning and would sit either out on our deck (I moved back home at this time) or near the window and have herbal tea and watch the birds. It was as if I was seeing this beautiful world for the first time. I became quite the observer in those months. I savored everything. Chocolate ice cream never tastes as good as when you are dying! It was as if all of my senses were heightened.

Some days I didn't feel well—those days I stayed in bed, but instead of being sad, angry, or depressed, I would take it like a lazy day, where you just flip through the channels and sleep on and off and do nothing but "veg." I had never allowed myself such luxuries before I was dying. I was always doing, doing, achieving, planning—always projecting into the future. Now I was just enjoying the moment. I would wonder sometimes what it was going to be like—you know, dying. What I would experience? I didn't really think much about after, just what it would be like to die. Is it like the lights going out? Like in the movies you sigh, look into someone's eyes, and fall over? I guess someone heard me pondering these questions in my head, because "help" was sent in the form of books and people—namely hospice—who helped me to understand the dying process. The man I had spoken to in Arizona called one day to see how I was doing with my new reality. I told him how I had done what he suggested and embraced my upcoming "transition," as he called it. I told him that I had a deeper connection to myself like never before and that I seemed to be getting unseen help from above. He laughed and told me how that has always been there for me—that I have always been connected— but I had not noticed. I told him that this dying process seemed to have freed me and I seemed to be more alive now than ever—could it be that I am healed? That my body healed too? He assured me that I was still on target to transit—not to let my false mind fool me or try and make a new interpretation of these events—but that I was spiritually healing and evolving. He also told me that one day, my process and what I experienced would help others. Part of this was to serve the whole. I didn't understand how that would happen if I wasn't alive to do it…but that wise man told me not to figure it out, just let it be. I thanked him for all he had done for me and for all he had given me. I felt the love and peace in my heart expand to him, and I knew he felt it too. He told me it was our destiny to meet and that I had helped him as much as he helped me. I knew I would not talk to him again after that—and I haven't since then, not even from here. There is no need to. I do hope he reads this though, so he can see how true his final words were (are) for me.

I died on a Tuesday evening surrounded by my family and friends. Those months, weeks, and days before I died were beautiful and sacred and filled with love. I got to do so many things and to experience all the pleasures of this life in that time. I got to say goodbye and make my final plans. I got to say things to those I love that I probably never would have said if I lived another hundred years. I even got to make amends for some stupid, petty things that had happened. I left completely free, with a full, loving heart. I left with the love and support of my family and friends. It was a beautiful transition, a beautiful new beginning into another life. I wish for everyone to die this way.

I hope this message inspires others to die with grace. If I had continued the "fight" I would have missed out on all of this. I would have lost the opportunity to really live. In those final months, I got more than I had ever wished for. I often "visit" those whose illness is the portal for their transition. Of course, not every illness is that, but for the ones that are, I am there, at some point, holding their hand, encouraging them to move into their truth—just the way the man did for me. It is the least I can do after what has been given to me.

With love and gratitude,

Lisa Ann

*

I used to volunteer with a hospice organization, and in hospice this is what we would call a good death—a beautiful death. It is where all the dots get dotted and all the T's get crossed. One leaves this world with no baggage and no karma—only love and peace.

I believe this kind of death helps those who remain on earth to find peace again. In her final time on earth, Lisa Ann became truly alive and present. Imagine living life like that all the time! I do hope her peace and acceptance helped her family and loved ones deal with her passing, or transition, as the healer called it.

While we are human, we experience death as a feeling of separation, but on a soul level, we *know* we are never separated—we *know* we are divinity incarnate. Maybe we can learn to accept death and release our belief in separation. Maybe we can remember what the soul already knows. Even though we may miss the physical presence of our loved ones, maybe we can learn to let go of the perception that they are somehow lost to us. There is a big difference.

Lisa was very wise and brave. The part of her that might have resisted this experience was nothing compared to the strength of her soul. Her story teaches us that there can be grace and power in the dying process by accepting one's destiny. Her death teaches all of us to live consciously. She reminds us that we do not have to wait until we are dying to live life fully.

—Ro

16
MARY

A Healing Place for Transforming Consciousness

There is a density in the energy connecting with me. It is a woman, and she is revealing some emotional and physical pain. Luckily, I am not feeling her physical discomfort before or during the message—I am just aware of it. Sometimes a medium, especially an empathic or healing medium, will connect to the physical, emotional, or mental sensations or symptoms of the person coming through. I have done this in other readings and writings and still do from time to time. Once I learned what it meant to be an *empath*, I could then use my empathic abilities to strengthen my mediumship and healing abilities instead of suffering with symptoms that were not mine.

People who are empathic can and often do connect to others—dead or alive—by taking on their physical, emotional, and mental pains. It can make for a great deal of confusion and discomfort until it is understood. Empaths are healers. They do not take on suffering intentionally, nor are they supposed to hold on to or own the symptoms. They are supposed to use the symptoms to gain information and then release whatever it is they pick up. Empaths are often unaware they are empathic. It is a soul's choice to come into this world with strong empathy, and it is a path of high service to spirit. If you suspect you are empathic, one good rule of thumb is to ask yourself, whenever you suffer from anything at all, "Is this mine?" If it is not, it will immediately subside, and you can then release it to spirit for healing. If it is your "stuff," it will stay and allow you an opportunity to understand its message or purpose in your life.

We are all empathic to a certain degree, but for some of us, empathy is our path and our power for healing. For some, it is part of the life's purpose. It is of the utmost importance to understand what empathy is and how it works, so you can manage it instead of it managing you. As always, staying aware and connected to your true *self* will help you know how empathy plays a role in your life.

*

I have that nauseous feeling again—the kind that comes on like a wave, like a dark cloud coming over an otherwise blue sky. It overtakes me and then the thoughts: *Oh no, please don't let it start. Please don't let it be as bad as the last time.* These are my memories from the time I was ill. I can still feel them even though I have long ago left my physical body. The trauma of the experience still remains, and sometimes I open it just to remember, and sometimes it unconsciously surfaces. Death does not always liberate you from the pain. It should, but it all depends on "where your head is at." Mine, I guess, still likes to visit the pain. They tell me that I have gotten better since I arrived here— that I don't "dwell" as long or often in the pain thoughts. They tell me I recognize them when they arise; I choose to change them—well, sometimes I do, at least. I think I should have gotten this shift while still on earth, but they reassure me it does not always happen there or here—but it always happens. The "they" I refer to are the beings of light that help us always. I was not aware of them at all when I was on earth, and it took a while for me to recognize and acknowledge them in this dimension. I'll admit, it was easier to open once I crossed from the physical plane. It wasn't as heavy. I didn't feel the weight of fear the way I did when I was physical. I could find peace inside my mind…but my mind was not completely open and ready. When I first left my body (and I did so with tremendous fear and a sense of loss of control), I felt completely light and free. I felt like I was ready and excited, but I didn't know for what. I noticed for the first time that I was not afraid and that I actually felt peaceful. I noticed there was a part of me that was not present—the part that lies to you, the part that had lied to me my times as Mary. I suddenly felt like myself, only I did not know who "my self" was. I found myself in this beautiful garden filled with every color rose you can imagine. The fragrance was overwhelming, and I was intrigued by the many colors and sizes. It was if the roses were humming. There was what I sensed an energy coming from each one and from this place that I had never experienced before. It was the most magnificent and breathtaking place I had ever been to. Two women greeted me here. I had enough sense to ask if this was heaven. I knew I was dead, but everything, including me, felt so real and alive. In fact, I don't remember ever feeling this alive when I was alive. I and everything around me seemed to be magnified (if that makes any sense). They assured me I was in the dimension of spirit and that they would help me to understand. They introduced themselves as Mina and Rose. I realized somewhere in my mind that my great grandmothers were named Mina and Rose. These ladies were young, not grandmotherly though—I was confused. With me explaining this, they knew and again assured me they were indeed my ancestors—their words—and that I would understand everything soon enough.

I was taken to a beautiful cottage at the edge of the garden. There were other women there and other "ancestors" attending them. Some felt familiar to me, although I did not recognize anyone. It all felt so loving, nurturing, and inviting. I felt a connection to everyone there even though I did not know anyone. We all felt like one being, yet separate. The time I spent there was wonderful. I was tended to in every way: physically, emotionally, mentally, and spiritually. It felt like a retreat of some sort where you are just pampered and loved. It was not what was done for me or what was said...it was the energy with which things were done and said. We were being filled with love. As we reached our feeling point, we would be allowed to move on. New women arrived every day, and after a while you could see how depleted they (we) were when we arrived, and how full we were when we left. Everyone filled at their own timing and to their own need.

When it was time for me to move on, I was brought to see my mother. I encountered a beautiful young woman who I instantly knew was my mother. Our encounter was filled with love and peace—very unlike our relationship on earth. I soon reconnected to many of my family members and friends...one of which was my brother, who had passed before I was born. I instantly knew him and felt great love for him even though I had not met him on earth. In this dimension you know someone by how they feel—by their essence. There are no thoughts, perceptions, or interpretations about this—just connection, just love. Some have a stronger love essence than others, and those are the ones you want to be around all the time. Just being around them makes you lighter, freer, more loving. It was explained to me that this happens on earth as well but that we do not operate from this place of knowing—we operate from what the mind tells us, and the mind is often controlled by the unconscious, false self, filled with fear and misinterpretations. No wonder things get so messed up there.

I am still in the process of learning many things here. Mina and Rose still help me expand my understanding of it all. I still visit the cottage for restoration and tranquility—especially after I have a thought like in the beginning, where I reach for the pain and fear. It feels more and more foreign and confusing than it used to, but there is still a part of me that chooses to go there. When I recognize it, and I do, I visit the cottage where the energy of love and nurturing is so strong, it helps me to hold the love and peace that I have expanded within and forget the pain and fear. My message, to anyone on earth who is like this: ask to be taken to the cottage during your dream state. Even if you do not remember it, you will be taken there, and you will be healed. Life on earth will improve dramatically for you—I promise.

I guess this is why I was asked to speak to you—so you could know there is help available. It is always available, whether you see it or believe in it. Just ask. I had to physically die before I knew this. I suffered and caused others a great deal of suffering because I did not know. Through the love and light that now fills me, I deliver this opportunity to you so that you may awaken and suffer no more.

It is my greatest honor to share this story with you. I do hope it helps.

With love,

Mary from Cincinnati

*

Mary's story is almost in direct contrast to the experience Lisa Ann had with death. Clearly Mary is still working on raising her consciousness while in spirit. Her entrance into spirit awakened her awareness, and that is her greatest tool. In her new afterlife she is healing what she could not in her physical life.

Mary tells us we can all find freedom and peace in visiting the cottage during our dream state or meditations—that we do not have to wait for death to access this space. Her story offers us an opportunity to access healing from spirit whenever we need it. For those who suffer from depression, illusions, delusions, anxiety, and fear, or for those who have isolated themselves in limiting mindsets, this may be especially helpful. Maybe Mina and Rose will greet us!

—Ro, written July 26, 2012

17

ALICE

A Description of the Dying Process

I seem to be most attuned to women in spirit right now. They are definitely the loudest and clearest at the moment. The woman coming through today, Alice, is not present in the room with me. Instead, I hear her voice in my head. I hear her speaking to me. This is how mediumship first began for me—through the channel of telepathy and clairaudience, which is the ability to psychically hear, receive, or transmit thoughts, words, and communication through the mind. It is still my strongest intuitive portal. I know very clearly when I am receiving information instead of creating thoughts with my mind. I know when I am hearing my own voice and when I am hearing the voice of others. It is through the practice and training of the mind with meditation that one can be clear about this. The practice of meditation is essential for anyone who does this work. Whoever decides to develop these abilities must have a very clear and strong mind (mental) field, a sturdy and grounded emotional center, and a physical structure or body that can handle the energetic dynamics needed to navigate the currents of psychic, intuitive, and mediumistic vibrations. One must also have or develop a very clear sense of *self*. It is imperative to know where you end and everything else begins. Due to the level of vibrational energy coming through, this ability could easily take a toll on one's mental, emotional, and physical containers if they are not strong enough to hold it. It is even more essential that the medium or psychic has done their own work and comes from a place of clarity and not from their wounds, fragmented pieces, or ego, otherwise the information coming through and the whole experience of mediumship will be tainted and filtered through the wounding. There is a term for this, referred to as the "wounded healer." It is best if these skills are handled by someone who is firmly in their power and who is mature enough to handle the responsibility of this work. One has a duty and responsibility as a medium to ensure that they are grounded and centered so their mediumship creates healing and not harm—to themselves as much as to others. If these abilities surface before the medium is ready, he or she can always decide to put them on hold and work on their *self* first. Simply say, "Not now. I am not ready, spirit, but please make me ready to handle this responsibility." It is important to know that we are always in control of our self and the mediumistic or psychic channel. We can shut it off or slow it down. We can learn to manage it so it does not manage us. It always comes back to knowing your own self. The spirit always seeks wholeness in mind, body, and heart. This is the most important task for all of us in this and every other lifetime.

*

My name is Alice. I come to speak to you about my physical death and what I experienced. Many people want to know what it is going to feel like to die. I believe the experience is different for everyone, depending on your state of consciousness, your belief system, your faith, trust, surrender or lack of, and most of all the level of density of your fear energy. But there are similarities I would like to touch on. First, there is awareness in the personal consciousness that death is impending, up to one and one half years before actual physical death. This is true even for those who die a sudden death. It could be a tone taken in the dream state, an actual knowing, a state of anxiety (not that everyone who feels anxiety is about to die; please do not misinterpret that), and a sense of change that seems confusing yet exciting. There may be a state of reflection that the individual may not be accustomed to. There may be signs, symbols, visits, messages from angels and guides (all of which usually go completely unnoticed except by the most astute, I might add), or a signal that states the hourglass has run out of earth time. Most people allow this clarity to pass them completely by. After all, it is a much evolved being that can face physical death knowingly and not try to alter the outcome. Some actually do face impending death square on, and let me tell you, those are the people you want to remember and even be around if you can. Those around someone who is getting ready to pass can often sense it too, and if you think the person getting ready to transition dismisses this intuitive information, it is nothing compared to what those that love them do. We as humans try so hard and resist what is such a natural process of life, and yet in the end, we all will go to the next chapter of our story; we will all make that transition from the earth plane to another. When someone is in the active part of transition, whether through illness, sudden trauma, silent trauma, or other, the conscious mind goes into what could be described as a dream state. It is like being asleep, feeling asleep, thinking you will awaken—and you do—only when you awaken you are in a new reality. The denseness and heaviness (some call it the negativity) of earth is no longer present. It is like you can finally think clear in your mind. Your physical body remains but feels completely alive, vibrant, and enhanced, and there is no emotional density. There is the presence of love energy in you, around you, from you. Some would describe this as bliss. You retain all of your memory of the earth experience and actually reclaim memories prior to the earth incarnation that may have been long forgotten. There is no emotional charge to these memories; they become neutral information. The first thing you notice as you become conscious to your new dimension is the overwhelming presence of love being directed at you. There is no density coming from you or around you to prevent you from feeling and knowing it like there is on earth. We usually individuate this love energy into "forms" that we recognize, so that we may comprehend it better. These forms take on the shape of our loved ones (on earth or in the dimension of spirit)—those we have revered as master teachers, angels or master presences on earth, animal forms, or just about anything that represents the energy of love to us. Since there is no dense "belief" of separation, those that transition feel, see, sense, and know the presence of their loved ones whom they supposedly "left behind" on earth. We respond to the call from earth through the consciousness of separation and are continuously trying to heal that thought form through what you call "spirit communication," but let me assure you, we feel no separation, because there is none. I know these concepts are hard to digest, but that is why I was sent to give them to you.

It is true that some take longer to get to this awareness than others. Again, since time, space, distance are only an earth-imagined thought, everyone makes this journey instantaneously and in the same way. Only from earth view would it appear that some take longer than others, or that some get stuck or do not leave the earth when their bodies die. That is really all relative.

I "died" when I was twenty-three years old. I was preparing for a life as a Catholic nun. There was an epidemic at the time of my death, and I, through my service-oriented life, contracted the illness and passed. I knew this was the path of my life. I always knew that this was how I was to die, and I never tried to resist it or question it. The ego would try and bargain that way; I was blessed to not have much of that. I embraced my destiny and willingly allowed it to unfold according to soul timing. I did not know when this would happen, but I knew to allow whatever my soul led me to. I radiated a grace from living in complete trust of my soul. Many thought I was perfect for the life of servitude I had chosen. Many could sense my spiritual connection and sought to replicate it themselves. I am very grateful for that. These same people could not understand why, in their eyes, my life was cut short. I could hear their words of despair and feel their sense of unjustness, pain, and sorrow at their perception that somehow, it was wrong for me to die so young, so good, and with so much to offer and so much more to do on earth. They could not understand what I had always known: It is never about that. It is about the soul's plan and individual destiny.

One year before I passed, I dreamed of the Archangel Gabriel, and she showed me a world that looked like earth but felt completely different. She asked me to visit with her there. Those dreams became more and more frequent, and I began spending more and more time in that dream state and in that world. As I spent more time there, I would awaken to earth dimension and feel disoriented and disconnected. It took me longer to get "acclimated" after I woke up. About a month before my illness, I remember looking at my parents. We were having dinner on a visit home from the convent. They were radiant. There was a power and presence around them, and I thought they must have surely been in a state of grace. When I returned to the convent that evening, I was concerned, thinking something may happen to them, that they seemed so "otherworldly" to me. I began to pray and ask for clarity to what I was sensing. The answer that I received was that my eyes were finally clear and I could see what I hadn't ever seen before but what was always right in front of me. I felt at peace. When I woke the next morning, I knew that this meant I was preparing to leave this plane. I just *knew*. For one moment I felt afraid, and then that melted into complete and utter peace. I only wish everyone could experience that level of peace while still on earth. I only wish that everyone could be ready to accept death the same way. Maybe this story is the beginning of that.

I was lucky enough to have a chance to leave the seeds of love and peace with all of those that I came in contact with right before I physically died. I did this through my words and actions, but mostly through my heart—that completely embraced the knowing of the impending outcome of my illness. People called me fearless after my death, and it is true—there was no fear present in me or around me as I passed. I would like to invoke that for everyone. Some thought my physical body was suffering through the illness and transition. Let me assure, I was not. The soul self never feels the physical impact of the dying process, no matter how traumatic.

I woke very quickly into my new reality. My mother, father, and all the children I had ministered to were there. So was Jesus and Mary and the face of God the Father…all were there to greet me, as this was my conscious creation of the love I felt. I have been serving humanity and beyond ever since. It has been my pleasure to connect to you today. I encourage you and all who read this to continue your good soul work on earth, and most importantly, to never fear the change you will all make from the earth plane. It is part of your sacred journey. May God bless you all.

*

What a powerful message from Alice. Her words and tone convey the power and conviction of a very enlightened being. What an honor it was for me to experience her and to be able to bring forward this very important information. Many people question the process of death and fear the unknown. I hope her message brings clarity and comfort to anyone who is facing death now or who may be afraid of dying. Her heartfelt encouragement to all of us is a testament to her continued work from spirit for humanity. What a blessing she is to all of us, and what a great service she has done by explaining what many people have questioned or pondered. Alice, thank you for continuing your life of service, even post death. I am very grateful.

—Ro, written September 20, 2011

18
LUCRETIA'S STORY

This story was written before *Speaking from Spirit* was even a thought in my mind. It was not told to me by Lucretia after her passing. Instead, this is my own personal account of my beloved sister Lucretia's passing due to colon cancer in 2007. I originally thought this would be published in a magazine, but of course, spirit always has its own purpose and timing for everything. This story seems fitting for the collection of stories composed in this book. Like Lisa Ann, my sister's passing was a good death. She left this world with dignity, grace, understanding, and plenty of love and support around her.

So many people resist their impending death, and even more fail to make peace before they leave this world. Cre—as we called her—faced her death square on, and in the process, she taught all of us how to make empowering choices, even when one feels completely powerless. I often told her she was amazing and that the story of her final weeks should be told—that it would be moving and inspiring to so many. It helped me greatly to write this story. It was very cathartic and helped me to make peace with the trauma I felt during Cre's illness and death.

Cre, this is for you. We will always be a team, no matter where we are. I love you.

*

We were sitting on the bathroom floor of my sister Lucretia's hospital room, too numb and full of despair to get up. Penetrating the room was the sound of the most beautiful gospel voice, singing "Somewhere Over the Rainbow." Cre peered at me through her pained eyes and told me, "Now I know it is true." The word *hospice* had taken a sledgehammer to any illusions she had of surviving colon cancer. The voice that carried the confirmation belonged to the lovely and compassionate-beyond-words nurse's aid who had been present for my sister during this last hospital stay and helped her receive the news that she was in fact dying.

The past eighteen months had been a long, arduous road. Diagnosed in February of 2006 with what appeared to be stage one colon cancer, surgery was scheduled for March 17. Then, days before her surgery, Cre's colon ruptured. Believing she had a kidney stone, she would not allow us to call her physicians. She held fast with her stubbornness and iron will through the most excruciating pain and our constant, distress-filled pleas. She was afraid they would postpone her surgery. I often feel cancer did not kill my sister—fear did. It was her fear that prevented her from seeking diagnosis and treatment all those months before—when she was bleeding rectally and reciting, "My stomach is bothering me," when asked what was wrong. It was fear that kept her from seeking another surgeon when the one she wanted wasn't available for a month post diagnosis. It was my fear of her—she was my older sister, the eldest of four powerful women, and the matriarch of our family—which prevented me from following what, was in hindsight, the wise thing to do. It was also my fear that prompted her to the doctor. For months I had been dreaming of her in a coffin and our family present while closing the lid. In the dream, I knew she had died suddenly of cancer. Being a lucid dreamer, I would think, *This makes no sense. Who dies suddenly from cancer?* Not understanding the dream, but definitely understanding my reoccurring feelings surrounding those dreams, I first encouraged and then bargained with her to go for a checkup, which eventually led to the diagnosis. When the surgeon returned from the operating room, speaking of a ruptured bowel, crucial twenty-four hours, sepsis, shock, cancer spreading, permanent colostomy bag, and a maybe a few good years…the vividness, meaning, and understanding of all those dreams hit me like a ton of bricks. Immediately, my human mind scrambled for assurance. *Is this what the dream was warning me about? Surely it meant something that she survived five agonizing days of a ruptured bowel? Did we prevent the outcome of "sudden death due to cancer" because we were aware of the cancer?* When my soul mind spoke, it informed me we had just received a miracle.

She couldn't understand why we were crying. Coming out of the surgery, she was by all means her clear, conscious, and in-charge self. She knew the scope of what had transpired, but what that meant had not struck her. I now realize her mind had a great way of filtering information and formatting it to her perception, instead of the truth. This was her blessing and her curse. I stayed the night, wanting to cling to her and to every second spent with her. We didn't sleep much, instead talking and holding on to each other all night. She was discharged almost two weeks later, weak and in serious despair. I thought it was due to the permanence of the colostomy bag she now had to wear. Maybe it was her soul mind, speaking over her human mind, that believed and trusted she would get better.

There were many setbacks in the six months of her chemotherapy treatments. She couldn't eat much and lost forty pounds. For an Italian American woman who was an incredible cook and who often showed her love for family and friends through cooking and dining out, this, I believe, was a fate worse than death. Her hair thinned considerably. She took this surprisingly well for a lifelong hair dresser. She was often nauseous. But the hardest part for us, her loved ones, was her constant pain. By the fall, Cre was showing improvement, and in November

2006, three days before Thanksgiving, we received the news via PET scan that she was now cancer free. We were overjoyed and contributed her miracle recovery to her strong will, her ability to endure, and the special assistance and help from my father and cousin Roger, who were now her guardian angels from heaven. We had a blessed Christmas and New Year. Her husband, George, planned a great trip to Aruba for the two of them. Life began to return to normal.

We celebrated our birthdays together like we did most years. Our husbands' birthdays were in late February, mine and Cre's early March. We went to dinner and ate like champs, so the next day when she complained of pain in her stomach, I assumed her body was still adjusting to eating solid, rich foods…or so my human mind fought to tell me. Still, why was I nagged by the memory of Cre's daughter Michelle announcing her second pregnancy and my sister crying uncontrollably? It didn't seem like they were tears of joy but tears of fear—or maybe knowing tears.

By April 2007 the cancer had reoccurred and spread to her liver. Back on the chemo she went, but this time nothing worked. It seemed she got worse every day. I knew in June that my sister was dying. No one else knew; the doctors were still talking treatment and recovery. It was like I was the only one who knew the emperor had no clothes on. I tried to reconcile what I knew to be true and what I wanted to be true. It was a constant internal battle. Her pain increased and became unmanageable. I was very much in charge of—had taken over—her care at this time. By the time we arrived in the hospital in August 2007, my worst fear was my sister would die before realizing she was dying and would not get to make her final plans or get to say goodbye. Bringing the truth to light would shatter her hopes, and I did not know if I had the courage to do that. Somehow, I managed to get the head floor nurse to bluntly tell my brother-in-law the truth: she had no clotting factor, her liver was failing, and there were tumors everywhere. This time, he heard it. I will bless this woman the remainder of my life for this great act of service. Michelle, George, and I were together when George broke the news to my sister. The sound of the song confirmed it. She went from incomprehension to understanding. The truth set her free.

Hospice care was waiting for us when we returned home the next day, along with food, flowers, gift baskets, family, and friends. Even our ex-husbands came. Hospice for my sister was like a constant party. I often thought people passing by probably thought there was a wonderful celebration going on in that house, when in fact we were preparing for the death of someone so important and integral to all our lives. For the next seven weeks, people came from my sister's past and present to be with her. They brought food and good wishes for us and a chance to say goodbye to her. Some days there would be thirty people at a time at this house. I would stand back and watch and think to myself that she was dying exactly how she lived. As weak as she was, she was completely up to this and would often control the shots from her now permanent position in the den. She would lovingly order—or should I say remind us—where the best dishes were kept, to put the coffee on, to vacuum, and to make sure the living room was presentable. She would also remind us to get rest and to make sure we ate—forever the caretaker, forever the nurturer, forever the control freak too! We gladly obeyed, knowing we would long for this once she was gone.

One night, while she slept, I observed a stream of spirit visitors coming to her and kneeling beside her. They just seemed to reach out and touch her, then move on. I did not know who they were, and at first I was afraid that maybe they were coming to take her. Then I noticed a woman whom I knew to be a very dear friend's mother. She had died many years before due to pancreatic cancer. I knew then that these visitors were souls who had passed from cancer and that they in some way were there to help her. The day after this visit, Cre rallied quite a bit.

We received many miracles at this time. In May, she experienced excruciating pain when she ate. She was put on a TPN line. We spent all those months watching the Food Network as she pined and mourned her inability to enjoy one of life's greatest pleasures. Within days of coming home on hospice, she began to eat again. She didn't eat much, but she ate whatever she wanted: chicken, lasagna, meatballs, watermelon, ice cream…and she ate it without pain. Her body seemed to rally a bit. Her strength seemed to come back. She brushed the remaining hair she had left and put on makeup for the first time in months. She held her grandson and fed him. She wasn't letting her fears and anxieties control her. She was embracing the experience and enjoying the moment without pushing it away. I reminded my family that this was not a sign of recovery, but of one who is aligned with their soul plan. My sister was back in her power in this very powerless situation.

She made her "death plans," as I call them—deciding to be cremated, what music to play and mass cards to order, who should speak, oh, and "Ask Father Randazzo to do the service and eulogy." She wanted us to hand out butterfly pins at her wake, in honor of her and her beloved Roger. My niece Alyssa teased her that we would be setting a trend handing out "wake favors." I intervened when she wanted George to go shopping for a new outfit for her to try on for her burial. I told her she would have to accept and trust his judgment. He would pick something nice. I also reminded her that she had beautiful and meticulously cared for clothes in her closet, to which she incredulously replied, "I am not wearing something old to be buried in." Yes, she was still very much Lucretia…and very much in charge.

It was a very sacred time. We were all there. Our children swam in the pool in the yard and would come in to give their beloved Aunt Cre a hug every so often. We would all have dinner together. We each had our roles and specific jobs to do. I stayed almost every night. Cre, my brother-in-law George, and I would stay up talking late into the night. It was a bittersweet pajama party. I was privileged to witness their most tender moments, like the night he recalled and recited every detail of their first date thirty years before. Their love and commitment grew stronger as she got weaker. They shared their last anniversary the week before she passed, with a beautiful candlelit dinner sent in by one of our dearest cousins.

She refused to use a bed pan. We would often sit in the bathroom in the middle of the night—her on the toilet, me on the floor—just like in the hospital. It became our magical confessional. We would talk about all sorts of things. Mostly we would be laughing and teasing each other. She made me promise I would take care of myself. I told her I would write this story, as no one would believe how she was "doing death." She asked me, "What will you call it? Your almost-dying sister?" Sitting there one night, she asked for a tissue. I assumed it was to blow her nose, wondering where she was going to get the strength to both pee and blow. Then, she bent all the way over and used the tissue to pick up lint in the corner of the floor. She looked up at my astonished face and simply said, "It was bothering me." One night, she reminded me when my father passed three years before. She asked me to promise that should anything happen to her, should she get sick, I would get her home, help her to die at home, and make sure she got to make her plans. I didn't remember this pact, but it was my father's passing that had led me to become a vigil volunteer with hospice. I was now at least trained for the task I had promised her I would do.

She made it very clear to me that while she understood and accepted what was happening, she would fight to the end. She would fight for every second of her life. She was not afraid of dying. She just loved the life she had and wanted to stay with it as long as she could. She worried for her husband and daughter. Her deepest regret was that she would not be here to be grandmother to her beautiful granddaughter and newborn grandson. She had so looked forward to that role all of her life. She knew I would not let her be in pain, but she did not want to be drugged up. Most of all, she wondered what it would be like. We talked a lot about what it would be like to leave your body and enter the world of spirit. She wanted to be awake and aware, and she wanted all of us to be there, even the children, if they could handle it. I told her I thought God would honor that for her. He or She did; all of her thoughts and wishes came to pass, I am relieved to say.

Football season started and we watched the Giants faithfully. To say she was an avid fan is an understatement—more like she believed and felt she was part of the team. She went through a terrible mourning, knowing she would never get to attend another game, that she would never see another season. That year, they won the Super Bowl, and I swear, she helped Eli Manning get out of that tackle to complete that miracle pass to David Tyree.

Things began to change in the beginning of October. I could sense the hourglass had turned over, but my human mind still hoped we could make it through the holidays. She was very agitated and irritable. She developed a cough and thought she was catching cold. I explained it was part of the process of dying. Her pain increased, and she fought the need for more medication, wanting to stay clear and lucid. I told her she needed to pray to God to help her to let go. She would have hit me if she could. Her vitals were slipping, yet her mind was crystal clear and sharp. She began to experience other dimensions. She would mention "seeing" our loved ones who passed, including our dad. I sensed them as well. We began to sit vigil—staying every night, watching her breath, taking her vitals, and most of all, trying to keep her comfortable. One morning I returned home to shower. My two youngest daughters approached me asking how their dearly loved Aunt Cre was. Telling them that Cre was actively dying now was for me the most painful part of this whole experience. They were devastated, and my body physically hurt for them. This was my sledgehammer, shattering all of my final shreds of hope. It was the last energetic straw that held her here. The truth was out once again. Her death was imminent. The following day, Monday, October 15, 2007, Cre struggled to live and breathe. She could no longer speak, but we knew she was cognizant and present. She began to shut down at 8:00 p.m. She took her last breath at 9:04 p.m., just as the Giants game was beginning. We were all there for her—every one of us.

My sister died just as she had asked for and planned. We carried out all her plans. George and Michelle bought her a beautiful pink dress for her burial. She would have been pleased. Eventually, we reluctantly went back to our lives, but there remains an empty hole. My mother has recently joined my father and sister, and so we have another loss to our family, another empty chair at Thanksgiving, another loved one to grieve. There are three of us left now. My comfort is that they—my mother, father, and sister—visit me often in my dreams. They are bright and healthy and young, and we hug and meet, always in a beautiful outdoor setting. They are happy, and that makes me smile. My sister lived an amazingly simple and grounded life. She died in an amazingly grace-filled way. I wanted…she wanted…everyone to know that.

*

When we suffer the loss of a loved one, we move into grief. Most people think of grief as a sadness or sorrow, and it is true—those are emotional components of grief. But grief is an actual state of energy we go into, like a winter, where we feel all sorts of mental, physical, and emotional symptoms. The body physically aches when we are in grief, and we may be more prone to illness as the immune system gets suppressed. We are lethargic, weary, edgy, and irritated. We may want to pull in and withdraw, much like a depression. We want to sleep and yet have trouble sleeping. We can't seem to find the energy to do anything or think clearly, and we may feel mentally overwhelmed and confused. We hit a peak at about the six-month mark, and then we may even hit a very angry state. We often reach for the emotion of anger over sadness. Anger is often a symptom of grief. Anger is a powerful emotion, where sadness feels powerless. We use anger to move us through grieving, to get us through—sort of like how caffeine is an energy prop that gets us through the day, especially if we are fatigued. The problem with anger is that we often misdirect it and use it to cast blame. We blame the doctors, nurses, each other, God, and even our loved one for dying. Anger walks a fine line of helping and hindering. It is healthy to feel angry in grief, but it is not healthy to live in that state. Left untreated, it will take a toll and eventually close our hearts. If it is directed inward, it can even make us sick. We have seen examples of this in some of these stories.

Usually, after the twelve- or thirteen-month mark post death, there is an energetic shift, and we begin to move beyond the grieving state. We may not move beyond the sadness, longing, sorrow, or sense of loss, but we do come out of the energetic state of grief. We may feel a return of energy, and hopefully we find a way to move forward with our lives—as life *does* continue on. Every death gives birth to a new beginning, whether we want it or not.

For some people it takes longer. Rarely does it take less time. We may feel guilty for moving forward, and we also may feel guilty or wrong for feeling happy. Sometimes we believe that we have to stay sad in order to stay connected to our deceased loved ones or that we are forgetting them or dishonoring them by letting go of some of the sadness. We think we have to finish being sad before we can be happy again, but we can be both happy and sad simultaneously. We do not have to wait for one to finish before the other begins. Some people vow never to be happy again once a loved one dies. Some people use the death of a loved one as an excuse to stop living, but our loved ones do not want this for us. All of the spirits I have ever met have had one universal message: they want their loved ones to be happy. They sometimes feel responsible when we don't. It is important to honor and understand grief so that we may navigate through it. It is an essential part of life, and we will all experience grief at one time or another. Working with it instead of against it will allow for a smoother transition for us still here in life and for those who have crossed to spirit.

Besides the grieving, we often suffer post-traumatic stress disorder (PTSD). This is very different than grieving, and we can get stuck here and stay traumatized by the death or events of our loved one's passing. We then relive every horror, every memory, every moment as if it is still happening. It is extremely important to work through the trauma. Speak to someone, write it down (like I did with Cre's story)…do whatever you have to do to process the trauma so that your energy is not frozen in time.

Grieving, trauma, sorrow, and sadness are all part of the living process. On this earth we experience love, and with that can come loss. As we learn to accept love and loss through death—ours and that of our loved ones, regardless of the circumstances or timing—we will always have peace in our hearts. This is what our loved ones in spirit wish for us.

—Ro

SECTION FOUR

STORIES OF THE DARK MIND

19

JASON

Transcending Addiction—A Return to Self

The energy vibration of the boy coming through to me today was confusing. On one hand it was dense and heavy, and then it would change and be light and bright. I did not know what to make of this, but after reading through his story, I realized I was feeling both the troubled lost boy he had once been (ego self) and the powerful soul he was growing into. I kept clearing my mind of any judgment and preconceived ideas so that I could stay neutral to these energies and be the clearest channel for his message. Long after we finished, I could feel Jason's presence in my writing space. I think he liked hanging around my home, feeling the presence of family again.

Spirit speaks about addiction as a path to emotional growth and enlightenment. Through the path of addiction, we have a potential for remarkable levels of emotional and soul evolution. The soul sometimes uses this path to accelerate higher states of emotional awareness and consciousness. Sometimes it chooses to experience a life of addiction as service to raise the level of compassion within the family and community and thereby affect the collective consciousness in a very profound way. It is easy while on the earth plane to get lost in the chaos of addiction and for one to lose all sense of self. Yet the soul often feels the potential is worth the risk. We will all choose in one lifetime or another to have this experience. We should hope to have the soul power, stamina, and grace to transcend it.

*

My name is Jason. I was seventeen years old when I OD'd. I was in my basement, getting high like usual. It was the same routine. I'd wrap the bandana around my arm and inject the tar in. Before I even finished, I was falling to the floor. It wasn't the usual feeling—the bliss, the escape, the transcendent high. From the instant it happened I knew something was wrong…. And then, I was out of my body. I stood there watching myself convulse, watching the foam come out of my mouth. There was blood dripping down my arm—the tip of the bandana mingling with it, the needle still dangling from its spot. My fingers turned blue; I thought that was odd. Then I realized I was watching this and wondered how that could be. My parents didn't find me until they came home from work. I stood and watched them cry over my body. I watched them as they agonized and then finally settled into shock. It took them a while to call the police and paramedics. They knew I was dead…. It was the shock; it put everything in slow motion. I stood and watched as the police questioned them. They truly believed that they didn't know I was a tar user. They knew I had "issues," but I guess their minds would not let them know that things had changed drastically one and a half years before. As soon as I started this stuff, I was a completely different person. They lost me then—I was an imposter living in their son's body. Still, they saw and believed what they wanted to believe…even though my behavior didn't add up to their vision.

I stood and watched them take my body away, wondering what was going to happen to it. I stood in the basement and watched my mother clean the blood that had made it to the floor, and then watched as she sat in the spot where I died, for hours, in what seemed to be a trance state…not unlike the high I was seeking when I put that needle in my arm. I felt nothing. I felt nothing when I was doing it… when I died…when I watched all of this…. Nothing, not physically, not emotionally…. Nothing. I just stood and watched.

After a while I decided to leave the house—I realized I could. I walked down the block of the lovely upper-class suburban neighborhood that my body had lived in. I walked into the main part of town. I walked to the high school I attended. I could see everything, feel nothing. Of course, no one saw me. I was dead and I knew it. I just watched everybody and everything.

The high school was somber. There was an announcement about my death. I was fairly new to the school—got kicked out of the private school I was in and had no choice but to go to this one. Funny, even when the school kicked me out because I got caught with a funny bag of dope, my parents still didn't register I was using. None of this is their fault though—it was going down this way no matter what, and I am just glad I didn't have to fight with them or do a stint in rehab that was not going to work anyway.

As I walked through the high school, I heard people talking. No one was surprised; everyone there knew what I was into, what I was about—kids always know. Teachers were whispering about what a shame it was, but still, they were not surprised. But I was surprised—I was surprised any of these people even noticed or cared. I made no effort to know anyone here. I made no effort to connect or interact with anyone anywhere, least of all at this school. I lived completely isolated from everyone in a world filled with people and things. From the first time I tried this drug, all I cared about, all I thought about, all I wanted, was it. It took the place of everyone and everything. My life became filled with motions just to get me to the next high. The only people I acknowledged at all were the people who could provide me with tar, and even *those* people I had only one use for. I didn't care about anyone, or anything.… Nothing and no one held any meaning to me. One moment, one decision, one action, changed my entire life. I slipped from life into a void. Even in death, I was still in that void, but now I was entirely alone because I didn't even have a need or compulsion for tar.

I continued to walk through the school, not exactly knowing why and not caring either. It never once occurred to me to wonder what was going to happen to me now that I was dead. I came to a classroom, and I began watching the math teacher giving the lesson. I became aware of a girl speaking to someone about me. I heard her say, "Please take care of his soul and watch over him, so he may find peace and serenity." As I watched her, I realized her mouth wasn't moving. She was thinking this. She kept repeating over and over similar words about my soul and love and finding the light within me. I didn't realize who she was talking to at first. I thought maybe she was speaking to me, then I realized she was praying—praying for me. I stood in front of her. She seemed to be paying attention to the math teacher, but her head was saying these things over and over. It was not beseeching; it was not emotional. It was clear and bright and just sort of neutral. I wondered why she was doing this—doing this for me. I never even talked to this girl. After a while she stopped, but it felt like the words she said didn't stop. Something began to change. I began to feel something, but I was not sure what.

Time passed and I was back in the basement. I began to get this feeling again, similar to when the girl was praying for me in math class. As I thought about that, I immediately found myself in front of church. My family was not of a religious nature, and the religion we were was not even Catholic. Still, I entered the church, and there was a teacher from my old private school in there. It was a Jesuit school I attended previously, but there were teachers that were not of the order. There she sat, rosary beads in hand, praying for the soul of Jason, asking for an intercession from God. I don't even know what an intercession is, or if there is a God, but here she is in front of me, saying these words in her head to someone, and I can hear them. Before I used, I had this teacher for Latin. I liked her. She pushed me to work harder in her class, and I respected her for that. I disconnected from her like I did everything else. I never expected her to be here thinking of me, remembering me, let alone praying for me. Again it was the same thing: clear, precise, with no emotion but great conviction in her words and energy. After she prayed for me, she went on to pray for others as well. I left at that point and walked home. I began to look around—at the trees, at the cars, at the people…. I started to "feel" something. I started to think…something I hadn't done in a long time. I wondered if the prayers or whatever they were was causing this feeling in me. Was this having an effect on me?

The next day, I returned to the school. I went to the math class and stood in front of the girl. She was just paying attention to the teacher. I waited for her to pray for me—she didn't. I kept going back there, and then one day, I thought, *I wish she would pray for me again.* As if she heard me, she began to ask—to whom I don't know—for my soul to be forgiven, for my soul to be reformed, for God to take me in his loving embrace. The words didn't register with me, but something in the fact that she said them did. I began to feel that feeling again—I began to feel. I looked around the room and asked these people, who I did not bother to know or care about in life, to pray for me. Most either ignored it or did not hear me, but there were two who did. As they joined in and sent a plea on my behalf, something dramatically began to shift in me…and it was as if their three minds synced up. Their words began to match, the energy became stronger, and things began to shift in me, in them, and in the room. They were not aware of what they were doing together or the effect it was having. I thought of my teacher, Mrs. M, who prayed for me in the Catholic church, and then I felt her praying for me—wherever she was—and I felt the power of her prayers join with the power of these three. I realized they were all different religions too. The girl who originally prayed for me was Muslim; the others: I am not sure what they were, if they were any religion at all. It didn't seem to matter. It didn't even matter what the words were. What mattered is that they were using their energy, their intentions, their minds, their *hearts*, to do for me what I could not, would not, and didn't know how to do for myself.

I did this for a while—recruited others to pray for me too. I whispered to my mother and father to pray for me. My mother prayed and would feel better. My father would start and then fall into such a despair, it would negate the prayer and cripple him. So I began to pray for him. And then I got the others to pray for him and my mom too. In time, I left earth and returned to spirit—more whole and healed than I had been in years. My mother and father began to recover and heal as well. I continued to incite the others to pray—not only for me and my family but for others. This is part of my work and mission in heaven, from heaven. Now, even my father prays and has no idea why he is doing it!

No one knew what they were doing or what effect their actions and thoughts were having. They did not know they were connected with each other—or with me. They did not know what we were doing, what we were creating together, or how they saved me. They do not know what we continue to do as a team of energy joining for a group cause. They just followed a feeling they had inside. They won't know of the great effort and effect they have been part of until they leave their body. You see, their efforts have not only affected me and others they have prayed for but have also affected them in the most positive way. I am so grateful to the girl who prayed for me. She has no idea what she has done—what she set into motion.

I was lost but now I'm found—I heard there was a song with these words in it. No truer words were ever spoken.

I will pray for you.

—Jason

*

When Jason spoke of injecting "tar," I was not sure if he meant that literally. I had to ask a friend if in fact there was a street drug with the slang name of tar. She confirmed that tar is a very deadly form of heroin.

What amazed me about this story is that Jason did not immediately find peace post death. He was not open to accepting the love directed to him while he was on earth, as he was stuck in an egoic state of fear, and even post death he had not transcended this mindset. Ultimately, his death did open him to the opportunity for that love to get in, as he was no longer influenced by the density and fear that resides on the earth plane and collective consciousness. He also received an intervention—a spiritual intervention—when that young girl began praying for him. She invoked the power of his spirit to make the shift required so that he could open to love again. She invoked a grace that allowed him to accept what was always available to him. In the space of spirit, which is a state of peace and pure love, there is no fear. It is easier to return to our soul power and to remember our divine self from there. Her prayers may or may not have been as effective while he was alive, but they would have helped in some way. While in spirit, and with the help of that young girl's prayers, Jason was able to break free of the ego lies that had shut him off from his own spirit and from God and love.

What immense power those prayers possessed. Her heartfelt intentions of love being sent on his behalf opened a space for his healing. The combined effort of love directed at him through group prayers helped him to transcend from this separated existence into his true form—a blissful state of love. Sometimes it takes a while, and sometimes we get lost, but Jason shows us we all return to love in the end. Imagine if we all spent time praying for each other? What a world this could be.

—Ro, written February 8, 2012

20
IZZIE

Finding Compassion and Love for Those Who Are Lost

There are so many spirits streaming into my room today. I wonder why so many are here. I immediately receive a response: "We are waiting patiently to tell you our stories. We have heard you will listen." It was on this day I realized the scope of this project spirit had given me. There are so many in spirit with so much to share with us—so many lessons and stories that can enrich our lives and make our earth experience even more loving, even more miraculous. And they need a channel, an accomplice, a scribe. Now, I don't always feel grateful for what people often call "this gift," but today I feel humbled to be chosen for this task. In this moment, I feel the sacredness of my life's work, and as I do, I am overwhelmed by the love and devotion pouring to me from all of spirit. On this day, my commitment is sealed. I will do whatever is asked of me so that these souls may have a voice on earth once again. I also realize this must be part of my contract with spirit and with these souls. It is part of my destiny to fulfill.

A woman steps forward at the urging of the group. She stands to the right side of me while everyone is sitting. She is standing, waiting for me. They have chosen her to go first, as their compassion for her and her story give them the patience to wait for another day, another opportunity.

*

My name is Isabel. I was called Izzie. I was murdered in my hometown on a crisp October night. I was coming home from work, parked my car in the garage at the apartment complex I lived in, when a man came up behind me. He just stepped into me and said, "Walk where I tell you to go." I was so stunned and just responded to what he said. The pressure of his body carried me along, and the next thing I knew, I was in his car—a car—and he was swiftly walking to the driver's side. It was one of those older model cars, and the gear change was on the steering wheel. It got stuck as he put the car in drive. Funny the things you remember. I was thinking to myself, *Why are you watching him do this? Jump out! Jump out!* but I was paralyzed. It didn't seem like he had a weapon; his presence, command, and actions were forceful enough to render me incapacitated. I now understood the term "frozen with fear."

He drove quite fast out of the garage. We passed a neighbor of mine—a gentleman walking his dog. He looked at me a little bewildered. Later he would tell the police about this encounter and give them a full description of the car. He was very instrumental in helping them catch the man who murdered me. He told the police something in his gut knew something was wrong, and that while he could not stop what was transpiring, he knew he should pay attention to what he could capture in the brief encounter. He said he had a hard time sleeping that night and didn't know why. On some level—maybe a soul level—he knew what was happening.

There was no talking in the car; I think my vocal chords completely shut down. I was so quiet, like I was trying to disappear into space. My mind was frozen too, which was a good thing. It did not allow me to wonder what would happen next.

(At this point, I notice many sitting with this woman, weeping—to me it feels like compassion emanating from their eyes. She notices too, and her compassion for them increases the energy in the room.)

We drove about twenty to twenty-five minutes to a wooded area. It occurred to me that people like him know these places—look for these places deliberately for just such plans. As we drove deeper into the wooded space, I started to panic. It felt like the worst anxiety—like a heart attack—yet still I was powerless to move or act. I realize now that flood of energy is exactly what should help you override your fear and make a bold, impulsive run for it—but in my case, I just got caught in more panic of how I was feeling. I thought I would die from this feeling—and that was the first time I realized I was going to die soon.

I won't go into the details of the assault and murder. Frankly, I wasn't mentally, emotionally, or spiritually present for most of it. One sort of "steps out of the body" when such trauma is occurring. I remember "seeing" people standing in the woods. They were watching and I was watching them. My back seemed to be to the scene of my body's assault. They walked out of the woods towards me. I realized they were not quite looking at me—they were looking at him, and there was deep sadness and compassion in their eyes, sort of like what you observed a few moments ago. It was then that I turned and saw myself lying on the ground, ravaged, naked, and staring blankly into space. My eyes were slightly bulging, and at first my face was very red—then it began to drain of color. My throat was bruised, and there was a little blood coming from the corner of my mouth. It was so odd; I felt nothing about this: not sad, not anger, not fear at all. I did feel compassion though—for the man.

A woman, named Rose, gently took my arm. She said, "It's all right. Come now. You can go home." We started to walk into the woods, which now seemed very illuminated and inviting. Each of the "people" who had been observing stopped and reached a hand to the

man, not to take him into the woods, but almost as if they were offering him something—some kind of energy, like love or compassion.
He did not see them, or sense them. At one point it seemed as if he
got angrier and was lashing about. He stomped my body at that point,
then left, and I never saw him again. Rose explained that they were
giving him a chance to remember and to let go of the hatred that was
blinding him, tricking him, and blocking his heart. She said that the
hatred makes one forget who they really are, and when one forgets,
one can do all sorts of hurtful things. She said no one was immune
to this—just some people forget more than others and then become
"who they are not." She says at every event like this, there are those
from spirit who come to offer help. I asked why they didn't help me.
Why was I left to die like this? Why did they not intervene? She said
the interventions go on for days, weeks, years prior to such events.
Some work, some do not. When individuals make choices that lead to
this, spirit's only chance is to offer another opportunity to help them
come back to themselves—return to right or sense, so to speak, to
reclaim their soul. It is harder afterwards because they lose themselves
even more in the action. I asked why was the compassion shown to
him and not to me—I was the victim. She said, "You gave him the
opportunity to come back to the goodness of his soul. Your soul offered him the chance to choose differently—it is the highest form
of compassion and love a soul could ever aspire to for another. Your
agreement with this man was on a soul level, not a conscious level, and
only those with the most pure heart and highest soul power can do
this. We do not feel compassion for you or need to; we honor and aspire to evolve to your level. You were always protected from suffering
and pain. Even in your moments of fear, there was calmness in mind
and heart as your soul self observed and comforted you. There was no
wrong on your part—not on any level—and in some way you knew
this…you knew this was part of your soul plan. We did not need to
help you; it is you who has helped all of us."

My parents were notified two weeks later that my body had been found. My death—the murder—shocked our small Wisconsin town. My parents prayed for the killer—prayed for his soul. I was so proud of them. They had taught me well. He was caught eight weeks later, partly due to the gentleman's description of the car. These were moments of intervention, as Rose had talked about. The man had the opportunity to rethink the situation, having been seen—he chose to ignore it. He still receives regular opportunities to "remember and return to soul" as he serves his prison time. Alas, he does not always remember. I visit him often in his dreams, not to haunt him but to offer him love and compassion. My hope is for him to feel this one day instead of the torment he continues to live in. I have joined the team that assists those who have forgotten who they are. This is what I do from my place in spirit.

Thank you for taking the time to speak with me today and for allowing me to share this story with your world. Call me should you forget—even if just for one moment—who you really are.

—Izzie

*

Izzie's story is such a powerful message of compassion. The words do not pay homage to the energy of peace and compassion that I could feel radiating from her. Who knew there was this team of spirits who try and intervene on our behalf? And just like on earth, some interventions work and some don't, but spirit will keep trying and will never give up on any of us. Izzie's soul had made an agreement to be of service to this man way before they were brought to this earth. Izzie's spirit knew the outcome may result in her physical exit from this world, yet she still chose to offer this man an opportunity to find himself again, to redeem himself, and to heal. What greater love and compassion could there be? Just knowing this level of love exists gives me a great comfort and heart healing. This story illustrates a soul's plan is always the path of love and service, even when the events seem tragic. Love and compassion of this magnitude transmute the darkness and offer an opportunity for great healing for this earth. Thank you, Izzie, for sharing your remarkable story with us and for allowing all of us to experience the depth of your compassion.

—Ro, written April 20, 2011

21
RODRIGO

Making Restitution

On this day, I am feeling relaxed, exhilarated, and ready to write. I hear the birds singing out my window. One of them seems to let me know it is time to write. I become aware of a young man who enters the space with me. He takes his place on the couch. He is thin, with dark circles under very dark eyes. He is shy and could seem a bit broody. His hair is short, dark, and straight and kind of sticking up on top. He appears Asian or maybe Latino. He is wearing jeans and loafers, a plain button-down or seersucker shirt with the sleeves rolled up, and a white tank top underneath. He has a scar on his shoulder, which looks a little jagged and thick, kind of like he was stabbed at one point. He waits patiently for me to take in his vision. His hands and knuckles have cuts on them, like he's been in a fight. In an instant the vision changes, and I see him wearing a bandana on his head. It covers his forehead—his third eye. It is red with some kind of white lettering. I open the channel by asking him telepathically, "Are you in a gang…?"

*

I was. I was killed by a gang leader in LA in 1997. I was seventeen years old. Had been on the streets since I was fourteen. My mother kicked me out, and I can't blame her—I was rough and angry and rebellious. I know I look sweet and innocent—shy like you say. I am also respectful, but when I have to be, fierce and brutal also. I was stabbed—many times. The scar you notice was from the first time I was stabbed. I was eight and it came at the hands of my stepfather. My mother threw him out. His parting words to us were: "He (meaning me) is scum. He will always be scum, and he will wind up dead sooner rather than later." They stuck with me. I took them as truth. Don't ask me why. It is not like I loved the guy or nothing or like I even thought he was smart. It's just when you hear something like that at eight years old, it has an effect on you—you believe the grownups and then you sort of envision this in your head, and it gets stuck there. It wasn't just the words, either; it was the whole scene and emotional energy of the situation. It sort of adds the "charge" to the words and the "scar" to the mind and heart. I had nice words said to me too—not by him but others—but there was no energetic "charge" at those times. I think that's what really makes them stick. Anyway, he was right, or I at least carried out the prophecy. I started to hang out with much older kids soon after that. I was eager to prove to them I was cool and tough. Soon they had me doing things I shouldn't, as "tests" to see if I belonged with them. I robbed an older woman of her pocketbook and ran away. I stole from local stores. My mother would ground me for disobeying curfew. She had no idea what I was doing when I was out but suspected it could not be good by the people I was with. I would sneak out the window at night. The more she tried to intervene, the more belligerent and defiant I got. Things graduated to dangerous by the time I was eleven. I was shaking kids down for money at school— that was all I really went for. I barely went, and when I was there, I hung out in the staircases, bathrooms, and hallways, where I could corner someone without anyone seeing. Remember, this was pre-9/11 and Columbine. School terrorizing was easy; even the older kids were afraid of me. Most of the time I didn't go to school. We had a hangout at an abandoned house six blocks from my own neighborhood. It had rats and big water bugs there, but we marked it as our territory and brought stuff in—junk, mostly, and some stolen stuff to make it our hangout. I was smoking cigarettes and weed then. The older guys thought it would be cool to see me high, so they slipped me X when I didn't know. Man, I was out of my mind feeling good. When I found out I wasn't mad, I wanted to try more stuff, so we did. I tried anything and everything. Funny, the one thing I didn't like was alcohol. It made me down, tired, and sad, and I didn't like that. Everything else—X, coke, freebasing, meth—I liked. I stayed away from anything that brought me down. By thirteen, I pretty much stopped going to school—was kicked out and punished when I did show up. Everyone knew I was bad news, so I just stopped going. I think they (school officials) were relieved. My mom was still on me. Sometimes I wouldn't even come home for days, and when I was home, I shut myself in my room and wouldn't talk to no one. I shared a room with my two younger brothers—they sort of knew the story and stayed away from me. I wasn't very nice to them. When I was home, they slept in the living room or with my mother. I just sort of ignored them all completely. I was into a lot of bad things now—worse than just shoplifting and mugging. I got pleasure in making people afraid. My reputation at such a young age got me an initiation into a gang. I did collections for "things." People were afraid of me just walking in the room—I was known to "go crazy" for no reason. I could just go off for no reason at all and start wailing on someone. I didn't even need to carry a weapon, 'cause when I got in that state I could really do some damage with just my hands and feet and whatever else might be available. At this time, my mom was at her breaking point—afraid when I was not home and even more afraid when I was. She kicked me out and told me not to come back. I laughed. I felt nothing then—I do now though; it catches up to you eventually. I think there might have been some part of me that was glad she kicked me out, sort of like it protected her and my brothers from what I had become, what I was becoming. I lived full-time at the hangout now—so did others. Things got much worse after that. I soon graduated to killing. My first murder was a retaliation hit for a rival gang member. Someone else was picked up for that even though the cops suspected me, and by street code—and fear—he didn't rat. I had been picked up a few times for minor things before this—nothing that sent me away for more than days or weeks—but now I was on the radar as a major player. Once you kill someone and get away with it, you get very brazen. At this point, we were just looking for people to mess up—to kill.

My death was retaliation—I was stabbed at my girlfriend's place. I was by myself—well, me, her, and her baby. None of my boys were there. It didn't hurt; I just was shocked they got to me. I actually believed I was invincible—even though I always knew what the dude said would come true. I remember looking at my bloody body. My girl was screaming, hiding in the closet—or maybe it was her baby screaming. They didn't touch them—just wanted me. I was just standing there—looking back and forth to my body, to her—not knowing where to go or what to do now. I was so calm and still, though my heart felt like it was beating—I hadn't remembered ever feeling that when I was alive. I was so peaceful and happy and didn't know why. I felt like myself—Rodrigo—for the first time since I was six years old. I felt like "me" again—whatever that really means. I wasn't sad anymore; I felt good. I've come to realize that anger and brutality sometimes are the substitutes for sad. Three people came to me then. I asked them, "Are you ghosts or angels or something?" They just smiled and said it was time to go. I was worried for a moment. What if they were going to bring me to hell? After all, isn't that where someone like me belongs? But I knew, somehow I knew inside, I wasn't going there. I was safe and I was okay—they were okay. It was like I was waking up from a very bad dream and was coming alive again.

Isn't that funny? I was dead and just coming alive. I wondered if those I had killed felt the same way. Just as I thought that they were there. Again, I got afraid, but something felt different; they weren't there to hurt me or punish me—they were just watching, and it was like they were sayin', "I forgive you." Then it was like I started to forgive myself. I didn't even know I felt bad about those things. When I was alive, on earth, I felt nothing about them. The three began to guide me out of the room. Everything got really bright, and then we were outside—but not in the neighborhood. We were somewhere I'd never seen, yet it felt familiar. We walked a bit, and then my granddad was there. I hadn't met him; he had died when I was little, but I knew it was him. He took me from there. I could feel his love for me so clearly. I don't remember feeling that on earth from no one, not even my mom—all I could feel from her was fear. I guess those were my angels, because when I left them I knew I could and would see them anytime I wanted.

We had some work to do. I had to process out all of the negativity from that life and begin to feel all that I had blocked on earth. I had to come to understand the choices that I made and how they affected others. I had to see how my choices impacted me—how they tore through me until there was none of the real me left. I had to make restitution to those I hurt. From this place, you do that by helping out the families of those you hurt while on earth. I am busy, busy, busy. I had to review all that I had done and all that I had felt. It is hard, but it is an opportunity to see it different. Sometimes I can, sometimes I can't. I am still working on that, still trying to grow and evolve, so to speak. I am not allowed back on earth yet—I think the powers that be don't trust me to not fall into the same delusion or to lose myself again. And I think they are right—I am not ready yet. I will be making restitution to families for generations just for that one brief life that caused so much pain to others, not to mention myself. As for my mother, she got her first moments of peace after I died. A calmness came over her. She shouldn't feel guilty about that; on some level it was her intuition telling her I was now safe—safe from myself and returning to wholeness again. I check in on her from time to time—my brothers too—but they are good. After my death, life opened up for them, and they began to thrive. As I shifted, they shifted too.

I look back on that life and feel bad for how lost I was. It didn't have to be that way—it is what I chose. I change it by changing now and living who I truly am, who I always was all along—love and goodness, divine perfection. I forgot, now I remember. One day, when I am stronger, I will try life on earth again, and I will do it different. I will create love and peace instead of destruction. I will hold true and remember.

The three sent me to speak with you today. They told me my story will help those who survive understand. People who live like I did won't get this, but those that know them will. It will help them—and allow me to make more restitution.

—Roddie

*

It is hard not to cry after reading Roddie's story. So much pain and hurt, yet through his death, he has come alive again. As he heals, he will be able to make restitution for his hate-filled acts and bring healing to those he hurt while on earth. He can attone for his actions by providing help from spirit to those who need it.

Most people believe in punishment for someone who has lived such a destructive life. Hell seems justified for someone who has caused so much pain. In all of us, there is a part that hopes someone like this should suffer. It seems logical that this will somehow balance the scales. Yet the power of love, compassion, and forgiveness is what is truly needed to heal him and ourselves as well. It is important for Roddie to reach a level of love and compassion for himself in spite of what he has done. We can help him and others like him as we learn to forgive and love him. We can offer him our prayers of love and forgiveness, and our heartfelt compassion in the hope that this will strengthen his ability to love himself. As we do this, we learn to love and forgive ourselves of any wrongdoing, and this brings about a great healing and shift for this world.

We create our own personal hell and suffering for things we have not forgiven within our own lives, past or present. Guilt and shame always seek punishment, and punishment is any pain or prison we create, whether on earth or in spirit. The concept of hell feels true for most of us, but the definition, description, and experience is different for each of us. Sometimes we create physical pain and suffering, sometimes emotional or financial.

Sometimes we create situations in which we feel trapped or imprisoned. I offer that all forms of pain or suffering on this planet have to do with unresolved guilt and shame, whether just or unjust, conscious or unconscious. How can pain, suffering, and punishment heal anything? Love is the only thing that can heal and mend these real or perceived wrongs—these wounds.

Spirit provides this unconditional love, allowing those like Rodrigo a chance to heal and come into wholeness. In turn, he can then atone for the wrongs he committed. Many of the other stories have said the same thing. This is true redemption.

I believe Roddie is trying to redeem himself and the consequences of his actions. Maybe as he does this from spirit, he will help those on earth who are struggling to do the same thing. Every time I see someone turn their life around from such a dark place, I will wonder if Roddie had anything to do with it. Thank you, Roddie, for sharing your story with us and for giving us a chance to see things in a different light.

—Ro, written April 27, 2011

22
EDGAR

Breaking Spells

This message was the third I had written since this process began, and I was shocked and a bit overwhelmed when I realized who was delivering this message. I have no way of knowing who will come through. I had sensed a presence with me all week, waiting for me to write. I felt intrigued by my mystery guest and was actually looking forward to this weekly meeting (writing session), but I was procrastinating a bit. I thought it was my false self or ego resisting the path my soul is (and was) choosing. When we are making progress in our spiritual growth and power, our ego will often try and divert our attention. It shows up as a fear, doubt, resistance, self sabotage, self defeat, procrastination, or diversion. These are all ego tricks and lies, and we need to overcome them in order to follow our destiny. I have set up with spirit—mine and divinity (God)—that should my ego (false self) show up with any of these tricks, spirit has my permission and approval to intervene on my behalf and redirect my energy. I realize this has been done for me many times without my approval, but as I consent I feel a level of confidence, safety, and security knowing I am divinely protected—especially from my own self. It is a way of surrendering more deeply to my own soul and thereby strengthening my own soul power. It gives me great comfort to know I have aligned so deeply with my soul and can allow it full expression in this world. You can do the same.

Spirit can be persistent, and my visitor was not dissuaded by my diversions. I finally got past my stuff, and suddenly the male energy I sensed wanted to give me some tutorial on the writing process. *Well isn't this interesting.* At first I thought maybe this was a guide coming to help me learn and fine-tune my writing skills. Maybe it was not something to be included in these fascinating stories. Never did I imagine I was getting an actual writer, let alone one of this caliber, coming through for me on this day....

*

I ask, "So who wants to come in and speak with me?"

And then I first hear dictated guidance on the writing process:

1. Center and clear your mind.

2. Approach it as if you know nothing...which you don't.

3. Call up the inner writer in you, not the scribe. The scribe takes the dictation, like you are doing now; the writer creates the story with words and images

4. Ask for help with this. Deceased journalists and reporters do well here—like Walter Cronkite.

5. Find tried and true resources and sources, and always refer to them—earth and spirit resources and sources.

6. Spirit will send you for writing classes later.

7. Show up at your desk regularly and consistently and you will develop a writing time and habit—it will allow you to be more creative.

"Is that it?"

"Yes."

"Okay, got it!" This certainly made things much clearer to me.

Now who comes in…oh my, my Dad is in the house, Ben Franklin, and…Edgar Allen Poe? Maybe for Halloween? Oh, wait—it was *he* who just spoke to me and gave me the tutorial on writing. I just got tutored by Edgar Allen Poe! Is there more? Did I miss something?

Edgar Allen Poe speaks:

My mind was always a little tormented; that is why it was so therapeutic to write those fascinating stories, as it purged them from my mind.

(I am thinking of my son Nick.)

He answers, "It is the same thing: his mind and my mind."

I reply, "Your stories were very dark in nature. Isn't it giving too much energy to the dark side of your mind when you entertain or focus on this?"

He replies, "It is a purge and gets it out of my head. To have it stay inside will make one go mad, implode, or act out. Your son has a strong spirit as did (do) I, so these writings I did channeled the impulse to the clearest place with least harm."

"Are you saying my Nick is the next Edgar Allen Poe?"

"He could be, or he could be clearing his head the way I was."

I ask, "Why did you come to me today?"

He smiles a wry smile and then answers, "Because you asked me."

"I did?"

"You asked for someone from spirit to help you, to speak to you, to create with you…. You opened your energy, thoughts, and mind, and I showed up."

"Why would you want to help me or create with me?"

"It gives me the chance to explore my mind in a different way—to utilize my talent of creating an image and picture differently. I am not as tormented as I was on earth. In spirit it is easy to be "light.""

"I see." I ask, "What do you want to create with me today?"

"I want to explain how my mind worked and how it has evolved…."

Edgar Allen Poe continues:

When the moon is lit in the night sky, you can see the distance as if it were close. You do not strain; instead, it pulls you in and mesmerizes you, making you want to jump there. You become the whole scene and transcend where you are, physically here and there. It is different than seeing it in the powerful light of day—when it is easy to be alert and distracted. The moon offers the glow and the shine, but also the darkness blocks out the distraction, allowing you to focus on what the moon has spotlighted. It is a portal which transforms your ability to travel in mind and body. Science looks for worm holes, and this is the key to it. As a child I was transfixed with this and tried to explain it to the adults around me. They couldn't see and didn't understand. I was isolated in my knowledge and understanding and lonely to have no one to share it with. I went inside to myself and created a world that transcended the one I was in—only there were monsters there sometimes, so I had to get them out to find the peace and solace I longed for internally and externally. No one could do it for me; I had to find my own way. It would not have been much different to have an external life that understood me—because I didn't understand me—and that was part of what created the external experience. I did not know at the time, I could ask for unseen help—to understand me, my process, my life, and my soul and earth experience. Had I known that, I am not sure if I would have even applied it—if I had, certainly I would not have felt so isolated, misunderstood, alone, confused. I would have not thought those things—been those things—therefore, I would not have experienced those things. My writings would have had happier endings, I suppose. The tormented would have found a way to peace—maybe that would have made for a better story. My stories are known as literary work—great literary work, yes, but dark, despairing, and hopeless. They incite fear and punishment, but they are created with genius and woven to capture attention and hold it. I am saying that a story of triumph after the fear may have brought the same recognition and the same power, but with a different reso-nance. I was destined to be a famed writer, inspirer, creator.... How I chose to do it—how it played out—could have been different. Yes, all because I forgot I was never alone. No one was there to remind me, because as I got deeper into the mindset, it would not allow anyone to break the spell. I could not see or experience anyone that would break that spell. Only death would do that for me. Some people do not even have death to do that…. See how easy it is for me to go to the dark? We all wind up in the same place though—returned to the "light" that I can guarantee—even if it takes a while!

*

I feel that what I just wrote was written as an interview. Just like in the beginning of my mediumship development, I asked a question and then heard him answer in my mind. My mind seems to link up to whom I am speaking, and their thoughts download into my mind. The information flows like a separate stream of consciousness. They, whoever they are—this time Edgar Allen Poe—are sending the information. This is different than, say, inspirational writing. With that, there is an inspiration from spirit, or a directive, but it is my thoughts and words putting together the information.

I notice there is a difference in the vibration of each of these writings and a different voice and style coming through. The very essence of the spirit connecting to me is embedded in the story. All of them are so different.

Most of this message from Edgar Allen Poe was about reminding us to open ourselves to allow help, support, and assistance—which is what he clearly gave me today. He also elaborates on how the false, fearful, ego self creates a distortion to our soul purpose, power, and destiny. The ego mind distorts how we see this world and ourselves. Ego creates separation, first from our self to our *self*, then from our source, God, creator, divinity, spirit…and then from others. Ego isolates; spirit unites and reunites. Edgar reminds us that ego plays with the mind and creates disillusionment, false perceptions, illusions, and delusions. I wonder if his willingness to tutor other writers is part of his healing so he can write from his soul perspective next time. I would offer on his behalf his assistance to all writers or those who suffer from fearful thoughts and delusions. Just call on him as needed. Wow…this is like having heaven in your back pocket. Think of the possibilities.

I think it would take a mind like his to see the opportunity presented in the portal he described. He obviously had a genius mind that could comprehend and see beyond the literal. It is also the same mind that may have created torment for him as well. Through his message he offers hope to anyone who may have such a mind, like any of the indigo children, now adults, who may walk that fine line of living between genius and madness. It is by remaining connected and reaching out that one will hold that line. Thanks, Mr. Poe, for the writing guidelines. Visit anytime with constructive feedback. I welcome being guided by the magnificent Edgar Allen Poe.

—Ro, written October 27, 2010

SECTION FIVE

STORIES FOR BETTER LIVING

23
ANNA

Shifting Consciousness One Mind at a Time

By the time I write Anna's story, I realize how fascinating this process has been so far and how much I have learned and grown. I can't imagine what the next story will bring, but I am sure it will be as inspirational and enlightening as the rest have been. Checking inward, I align and attune my energy so that I am ready to receive the presence of spirit. Next, I check to see if I am making a connection with anyone yet. I begin to sense the energy of a woman. This is done psychically, with the inner senses: clairvoyance, clairaudience, clairsentience, and claircognizance. Today my connection begins with a feeling or sensing (clairsentience), and I know I need to go deeper to get more information. We all have these psychic-intuitive abilities, but for most people they lie dormant, untapped, undeveloped, and often disregarded. We can all develop a stronger connection to these senses with practice, understanding, and patience. Intuition is the voice of our higher self—our spirit—and when we learn to work with our multisensory ability, we become more consciously connected to our spirit and to divine spirit. With time and practice, one will learn to trust their insight and intuition and to use these senses to navigate life and possibly to be in service to spirit.

Some people think of psychic senses as the ability to predict the future, but that is not what they are about. Our psychic senses give us greater insight and allow us to sense information that is not overt. Our fear of the unknown often prevents us from exploring this natural part of our nature, yet once uncovered, we find a depth to ourselves and an understanding of life that actually lessens our fears and anxieties.

Today, at this moment, I am using my psychic senses to help me connect to someone in spirit, but I will also use them when I am driving to sense the best route to take to work, and also when I am in the grocery store picking up produce for my family. As I explore my feeling of a female presence, I begin to sense she is frail in body yet strong in character and spirit. I am not sure what that means yet, so I move into my clairaudient ability and begin to listen....

*

My name is Anna. I lived in a time when women had very few rights and privileges. I was my father's daughter, and then I was my husband's wife. These were the ways I was owned; these were the roles I was born to live in that life. There were no choices—your choices were made for you by the men who owned you. If you were a complacent type, it was not so bad. If you were not, it was a living hell. I was not a complacent type. My father decided what clothes I could wear and what food my family ate. True, my mother prepared it, but my father decided what it was. These decisions were not based on what was best for the family—more, what we could afford, what might be available, and also what leverage it gave my father in life. You might wonder what kind of leverage one could gain by eating potatoes instead of, say, corn. Well, the leverage came in what you needed or could provide to the farmer who grew those potatoes and corn. Decisions were never simple; they were power plays that ensured standing and survival, sometime prosperity and position—if you were lucky. Not much has changed in your life timeframe—it may appear as if it has, but the undercurrents and undertones are still the same, only more covert.

When I married—at the age my father said, and to the man (family) my father picked—it was no different. Now my husband did the choosing, and I once again had to comply—and smile about it as if all was wonderful. Being born in this timeframe and with the mind, spirit, and personality I had was not easy. I realize we are sent into such situations and such lifetimes to start the change that is necessary. That is why my mind was so different than everyone else's. It was not an easy life. I was often beaten. My husband was determined to make me comply with his choices in whatever means necessary. I did learn to be more submissive—well, actually, I always submitted; it was the attitude, energy, and demeanor I brought to the submission that often got me in trouble. I learned to cover that more. But covering it did not mean I did not feel it…it was just inside. This choice (one of the only ones I had) allowed my physical life at least to be easier. It was the best choice in the moment and one that probably saved my children from growing up without their mother.

My outside behavior may have changed, but my inside thoughts and wishes did not. I could see that things did not have to be this way in life. I could feel my equableness to my husband even if it was not expressed or lived. I could know the injustice this was to every person—not just the women, but also for the men who carried out these intolerable beliefs and actions too. I also *knew* that it was inevitable that it would somehow, someday, change, just because I could see it, feel it, know it…. And that is what got me through that lifetime.

In your world now, there have been many changes in which you live the equality of the soul (human) experience that I was denied. There is, of course, more to come, as this is not a fully realized concept throughout your planet (timeframe). I would love to take sole credit for this, but that would not be true. There were more who thought like me before and during the time I lived. Some were killed and tortured for expressing their convictions—that is a story for another time. Some just suffered in silence. Me, I did not suffer as much, because somehow I knew the power of my thoughts were the catalyst creating the change, and that gave me great comfort and strength. I revisited earth life many times after my lifetime as Anna—always with a bit more strength and power to help create the mindset of equality of all. You have even read about me in history books. There are many more willing now to speak this truth loud and clear, as time, momentum, and shifts in beliefs have fueled this emerging reality. Still, for some, the consequences can be death or torture, but not as often, and that is definitely not as accepted or condoned. It gets stronger and the change moves faster. Equality is the cornerstone of the belief we are all one. We move closer to that reality with every thought, with every word, with every action that conveys that belief. Know your power to think this and feel this is so; it is a great contributor—in my life it was the only power I had, and look what it has done! Hold your thoughts with clarity; do not waiver from what you know are true and just. Do not be afraid to think beyond the current reality to what could be—you are helping to create it just by doing that. Own the power you have to envision a beautiful world, because it is in that power that you are the foundation for it. Do not let the current circumstances and reality diminish what you know to be true. Hold yourself, because the power of your convictions and thoughts does make a difference in this world.

With the highest regards,
Anna

*

Anna shows us the power of our thoughts and the effect they have on our reality. The effect is not always immediate, but knowing one single person's thoughts can and do change things is truly inspiring. She was shifting consciousness by holding, with certainty and conviction, trust in her inner vision—her intuition, her clairvoyant ability.

When Anna mentioned that she lived many lives with the same mission and theme, and that we had read about her, my first thought was of Susan B. Anthony and then of Abraham Lincoln. Perhaps she incarnated as these awesome and life-changing figures, or maybe she was just part of the same stream of consciousness that they were connected to. In order for their actions to have any power, a game-changing thought would have had to be present in consciousness first. There has to be an evolution of consciousness before there can be a revolutionary new reality. Anna certainly contributed to this. She also did not allow the limits of her lifetime to make her powerless. She worked within those limits to survive, thrive, and still hold her power. Even though she had to submit to the reality—or accept the reality she was in on its terms—she was able to hold her conviction and will internally. She seems to carry the energy of both the divine feminine and divine masculine in equal strength. It was certainly my pleasure to meet her. Anna, thank you for all you have done for women everywhere and what you have done for our planet.

—Ro, written February 1, 2012

24
EARTH SPEAKS

Clarity

Today I need to start with a very deep meditation. As I meditate, I feel as if I go into a space where I am beyond my consciousness and in the place of oneness with everyone and everything. I am not sure I want to return.... There is so much peace and love in this space. As I come back to the present moment, I have to remind myself to reground and connect to earth. It takes me a while to fully root back into my body. As I come out of the meditation I open my energy and connect to spirit. I am not yet aware of a particular presence with me, nor do I feel as if I am in the vibration for mediumship. Hmmm. I notice that my healing chakra has been activated. This is the chakra located between the heart and throat. When it is activated, it often means that healing energy from divinity is being channeled through—for me, to me, or through me for another. My root chakra, which resides at the base of the spine, appears in the color of baby pink. On the chakra wheel this root chakra resonates to a vibrant red color. When there is another color present, the energy and vibration of that color is influencing the consciousness and programming of that particular chakra. Baby pink often represents unconditional love and very maternal divine mother love. As it resides in the root, this vibrational color influences and enhances my basic, ground-level maternal energy, my sense of safety and security in this world, my connection to my own mother, my sense of support from my family and culture, and my connection and trust to life and living in general. Noticing this, I now feel firmly rooted and grounded to earth's core, completely safe and secure in my life and with the process of life. It is a very good feeling—soft, yet resilient and powerful. I follow this connection to earth and am suddenly aware of earth's spirit or soul. There is a tremendous outpouring of love and devotion coming into me from this connection, as if it travels up from an invisible umbilical cord that connects me to earth herself. I decide to dialogue with earth's spirit and see what she might tell me today. Through claircognizance—the sense of knowing—earth relays this message. She tells me she has completed a shift in energy, and as she settles with this, so do we with a grounded, clear force. She is conveying this information through the divine feminine aspect of divine mother. She also expresses her essence from the other two expressions of the divine feminine: the maiden and the crone (wise woman). Her nurturing energy is very strong and clear today, ready and willing to share with all those who seek her wisdom.

*

I ask, "Can we ask on behalf of someone else for nurturing energy?"

"No," she simply and clearly says. "You cannot do for others what they need to do for themselves."

"I understand."

Earth says she wants us to go outside and breathe deeply the air and life force available to us today.

I joke that I am in New Jersey and that this area is filled with so much toxicity.

She laughs at my worry and assures me that when we align with the pure air and vitality, that is what we will receive; when we align with the toxicity, that is what we will receive. "It is as simple as that, and it is with all things…. Align yourself with good and that is what you will receive and experience. Align with power, money, insight, health, accomplishment, peace—what have you—and that is what you will experience and receive."

"How do we align?" I ask.

"Simply through the mind and thought—think it and so it is."

"What about the heart?"

"The heart is always aligned with what is true and real."

"It is? How do you explain heartache? Or codependence? Or neediness?"

"They are not of the heart but of the mind. They are ego (mind) distortions that have hijacked the heart and turned it inside out. They are lies one believes and then experiences through the heart."

"So what do we do about that?"

"Stay clear in the mind, of course. One thing that helps that is going outside and breathing deeply and taking in the vitality. If everyone did that every day, for just one minute, your collective reality would transform dramatically."

"I am going to try that—for one month," I state. "From now until December second, I am going to do this and see what happens. I will put it in my newsletter as a challenge. I will record what shifts—if anything—and in a month report back."

"You doubt yourself (me) with this?"

"No, I am human and need to experience to know. Isn't that what I came to earth for—to experience? Isn't that my soul's goal?"

"Yes, but you say this as though you do not believe. Your soul knows it is true. The thing is, you experience what you believe and think, consciously or unconsciously, and so it is all experience, but your soul did not choose all the experiences; sometimes your limited ego mind did. It will be helpful for you to go outside with wide-eyed wonder, complete trust and faith, and hopefulness—not as a challenge, not with an agenda or expectation or doubt."

"And that is what is compelling me and exciting me to do this. I feel that I am not just speaking to earth herself. I feel I am in the presence of many women, goddesses, and masters who hold the divine feminine principle."

"You are correct—there is Kwan Yin, Mother Teresa, Teresa of Avila, Mary Magdalene, Dianna, Venus, Guadeloupe, Arta, Artemis, Aphrodite, Kali Ma, Shiva, and others present."

"I can feel the blend and hear the different voices of each of you."

"Each one of us represents aspects and archetypes of the divine feminine, and all of us are an expression of the earth power. Every man and woman holds each of us within them and can access this by intention and alignment."

"Say this in a way someone would understand who is not familiar with this concept," I request.

"Within you, you have access to everything you seek. Think it and it is there. Your mind may say it is not, but that is not true. And as you read this, your soul hears the message and *remembers*—once you remember who and what you are, you cannot *un-remember*. You have awakened. You can try and pretend you haven't heard or remembered, but that will be very uncomfortable. It is always that simple."

"So if, say, Congress goes outside every day to breathe and take in vitality, what would happen?"

"The same as what would happen to you: they would change and become who they really are, they would remember without being told who they really are, they would light the world with their soul power and be able to use their position and venue for good—as a means to express goodness and soul power instead of ego-driven behaviors and fears."

"We all go outside—most of us every day—even if it is just to go from the house to the car. Why then are we not changed?"

"Because you have not gone outside with the intention of breathing and taking in vitality and life force. You have been unaware it is there; there has been no conscious link. Once the consciousness aligns, intends, and asks for this, it is apparent, and everything changes dramatically."

"I am going to tell everyone this."

"You absolutely can and should—it is the intention of this writing; however, hold no expectation. Everyone will "hear" it, but the ego of some will get in the way of activating it. Still, the information will have been provided, and the opportunity will remain present (dormant) in each person, in their mind. When the ego has weakened sufficiently and personal power has been reclaimed, the soul self will activate the action, and there the change occurs."

"It sounds so simple and so hard."

"It is only hard because humanity thus far has made it so. It will not always be that way. It is not that way everywhere—only here, only now."

"Is there anything else you would like to say, share?"

"No."

"Thank you for coming today and for presenting me with this very helpful information. I am grateful and hopeful."

*

Well! We have been told, no? What a compassionate, clear, wise message delivered with a healthy dose of unconditional, nonjudgmental love. Could you hear and feel the difference in the energy when all of the goddesses were present? What if we all took this advice and spent time outside absorbing the earth vitality? How might that change us and our world?

This information came through claircognizance—meaning I received knowledge or information I would not normally have known or had previous knowledge about. With claircognizance or clairknowing, spirit impresses us with a truth that seems to pop into the head and heart as a full concept or knowing. It feels like a complete awareness of something where there was previously none before.

I am not sure what to write after this message. I think I have to digest all of this information. I know I especially need to pay attention to the part about loving in a clear way and surrendering my fears that might create an obstructed form of love.

April 21, 2012: It is Earth Day tomorrow, and something or someone reminded me to review this story before I prepare to go out and lead a yoga-in-the-park class. After I wrote this message from earth, I consciously paid more attention to being connected to her when I was outside. My daily walks took on a completely different feel and meaning. My body felt better than it had in years. There was a fluidity and sensuality to my body that stayed long after I returned indoors. Now I know why domesticated animals long to be outside and often look out the window. Earth and I have now formed a deeper, more intimate connection after this writing. I now have a reverence for her and for life that is completely different. And she was right: my energy, my power, my clarity, and my emotional energy completely shifted from this change in intention and consciousness. This may not be news for some people, especially gardeners or outdoorsmen, but for me it was "earth-shattering" info!

Remember to set the intention to connect with the vibrance and let go of any fear of the toxins in the environment. Greet the trees, grass, flowers, and animals that you meet in your outdoor encounters. Take in every breath, sight, sound, and feel. Absorb it all through your heart, and watch your body and your life transform.

—Ro, written November 1, 2010

25
A CHANNELED STORY

Spirit Speaks to Us

I have no presence or spirit with me today. The room feels empty except for a sort of electricity in the air. Maybe I am not supposed to write? Maybe I need to go deeper into my meditation? I get very still and quiet. Soon I am guided not to panic. The energy created when we panic stops the flow of information and connection. I begin to relax, and with that I become clear and begin to write whatever comes into my mind and heart. I feel the buildup of energy that comes when you are about to receive a knowing. It comes very quick and fast, and it comes as a complete thought. Anyone who has ever done automatic writing knows how fast and fluid this is—almost as if you cannot keep up with the flow. When the download is complete, the writing just stops.

Automatic writing, or psychography, is when the writer puts his or her own mind to the side, and through the observing self, channels the information given from the higher self or from the ascended masters or guides—all of which are forms of divinity. The writer is not creating the thoughts from the conscious mind; the thoughts are coming from another source, without conscious awareness of the content. The Bible is one of the best examples of a channeled book. So are *A Course in Miracles* and *Conversations with God*. In a way, all of the stories written in this book are channeled—as they have come from a spirit that has left this physical world. But this day was very different, and there was not a specific entity coming through. Instead, it was a knowing coming from a source of very deep wisdom....

*

Heartbreak is a very hard thing for humans to deal with. It can turn their thoughts cold and leave their bodies empty and depleted. The heartbreak a mother bears when she sees her child's limits and can do nothing about them.... The heartbreak of losing a loved one—anytime, anywhere, anyone.... The heartbreak of experiencing something completely out of your control, through no fault of your own, that has devastating consequences for your life, for the rest of your life.... And then there is the self-made heartache—the kind that comes from attachment to an outcome, a desire, or an expectation. While these are felt and experienced the same way as the former, these can be even more dangerous as they incite the ego into response. It is true that all experiences can be brought to the soul or the ego, and both will have different interpretations. The human self will experience a reaction to events, but the soul or ego will determine the reaction. It is the latter that has a greater chance of succumbing to ego interpretation and response because it is based on ego in the first place.

We have talked about those who have taken adversity and heartache and used it to align with destiny and bring message, change, love, and hope to our planet. History books are full of these people—full of their stories. One repeated often is Jesus' story about love and forgiveness. His ego could have certainly run amuck through his life, and most certainly his human self was at least uncertain and apprehensive when confronted with pain and suffering. His could have easily been a different story told all these years later…not unlike the one told about Adolf Hitler, whose ego made the choices and produced the outcome. All choices and actions come from one or the other—truly there is no neutral point—and with that, the effects either influence more soul power or ego strength. This, of course, is reflected in the world we then create and live in. All choice eventually springs from heartbreak of one kind or another. The heart feels it first; the head then takes over. The heart is either aligned with the head, or the head is aligned with the heart. If the heart is aligned with the head, the head's interpretations are going to determine the degree to which the heartbreak will be felt, how long it will linger, and how much clarity can be achieved. Clarity will only come from the head aligned from the heart, because in the heart is the energy of love among other virtues that will allow the head's thoughts, perceptions, interpretations, and such to remain clear and true. It is important to note that one does not overrule the other; it is in the harmony of both that peace can be found, but which comes first is of significance, because leading through the head is tricky, and backpedaling, so to speak, is often required.

It is easy enough to say that this life is all an illusion, that all suffering is an illusion, and that there is nothing but love.… But living the experience of this is trickier than just knowing this to be true. So as one experiences the heartbreak of anything, one needs to step back, step into themselves, and completely align with soul. At the very least, become aware of self so that if you fall prey to ego interpretations, it can be recognized and damage control (and it will be needed) can begin. If it is at all possible, work all the time to keep the head aligned with the heart. Move to the rhythm of love in all of your life. Surround yourself with those who do this and places that exude this. Feed the love inside of you, not by doing or giving, but by receiving and being. You know it when you feel it—exclude that which produces no love.

This would be the message that we give to earth-inhabiting souls at this moment. *We* speaks of the many voices, both individually and collectively, that you call loved ones, angels, guides, and teachers.

Let the head align with the heart. Let actions come from soul. Allow choices that create peace. And so it is.

AND SO IT IS.

—Ro, written January 26, 2011

CONCLUSION

From what I have learned through mediumship, we come to this life, body, and world as a perfect, divine-soul being with a purpose, plan, and destiny. We are designed to grow and evolve into higher states of awareness and consciousness. As evident through these stories, in our humanness we make mistakes. Sometimes we get lost or life becomes so hard we lose our way or ourselves. We waste energy living in the past, or with emotional regret and guilt. We forget how perfect and divine we are. When this happens, we live from this disconnected place and create a life (world) of chaos and suffering. We perpetuate a cycle of the suffering and contribute to an ego-created world. Yet it does not have to be this way. There is a quote: "To err is human, to forgive, divine." Forgiving the self is often harder than forgiving another. When we lose our compassion for ourselves and for others, we fate ourselves to struggle and suffer. We then contribute that to the collective consciousness as well. I believe by sharing their stories, these spirits are assisting us so we can move past this and into a more joyful and peace-filled existence while on earth. We do not have to wait until we die before we "get it."

These souls really want us to remember how divine we are. They want us to remember who we are at the core and that what we are experiencing in the moment is just a story. They want us to know that even when we make a mistake, and we will, we are still perfect and still divine. The most important thing is to learn from the mistakes we make and to grow and move forward.

So how do we consciously stay connected to our spirit? How do we grow and evolve our spiritual nature so that our physical, emotional, and mental parts become an expression of our spirit instead of fragmented, disconnected pieces we live from? It is done by coming from our heart of love and compassion. It is important for us to consciously remember that we are spirit in a body—that while we think, we are not our thoughts, and that while we feel, we are not our emotions or our bodies. We are so much more. When we identify with our spirit first, we can then recognize everyone else as spirit also. In that realization there are no differences and no separation.

Our true essence is pure love and joy. Just like a newborn who comes to this world perfect, we are this perfection and joy even when we are not acting perfect or joyful. In those human moments, we have just forgotten who we truly are.

It is also essential to feed the spirit and grow its strength and power. There are three branches that encourage this growth: practice, service, and study.

Practice is anything that brings a sense of peace and inner connection, such as prayer, meditation, yoga, ritual. It can include nature, solitude, or any hobby or personal passion that brings one into a deep communion with self and divinity, such as gardening or exercise. It is in our daily practice that we connect deeply to our inner voice—our higher self.

Service is anything done mindfully and intentionally from your best talents, skills, gifts, and abilities. Service can be done with pay or without, but it is the thought that what you are doing and what you are contributing is coming from your best self and is somehow benefiting this world. Service is an intention. Your service contributes to the greater good, and it shows a reverence for self and others.

Study is anything that expands the mind and increases knowledge and awareness beyond a current frame of reference. Study can include spiritual and religious teachings, but truly anything learned beyond the limits of one's personal experience opens the mind and heart and connects us to others.

Practicing these three branches feeds the spirit and strengthens the collective consciousness in a very positive way. When we live our most authentic life and live from our truly authentic self, we strengthen the collective soul. We live in soul power.

While we all have the capability to see beyond our earthly experience and to perceive this world and our lives through the intelligence of our soul, not all of us do. As some of these stories have shown, we may not get it while we are alive, but we eventually get it. This world has been in a perpetual cycle of ego creations. I believe we are at an unprecedented time where we are being called to create heaven on earth, and we do that by creating from our soul instead of creating unconsciously through our wounds or fragmented self. These stories—all of them—repeat over and over that the only way to shift, change, heal, and grow is to return to love, to come from love, and to create from love. We are not meant to suffer. By design we are meant to enjoy—because we *are* joy. It is time. Let these stories show us how.

—Ro

ACKNOWLEDGMENTS

First—thank you, God, for my life and the ability to live it.

I want to thank all those who have come from spirit to share their stories. I know there are many more waiting to tell this world what they have experienced and what they have come to understand. Every day, I feel the complete love and support of all those who are in Spirit, standing with me, encouraging me, loving me, and guiding me. I am grateful and humbled by your power and grace. Thank you to all those I have met since you left earth. I feel you are now my friends, and I know that when it is time for me to join you in spirit, you and my family will be there to greet me.

I want to thank my children—Nicolas Joseph, Justine Marie, Julianne Rose, and Grace Anna—for choosing me to be your mom on this journey. It has been my highest honor and greatest achievement. You ground me and hold me and give me a reason to be a better person. I am so glad we walk this life together.

For my husband, John, my partner in this life and every other; I only became *me* when we became *we*. In the safety of our love and connection, pieces of me emerged that I did not even know existed.

I have never felt so complete until I met you. Thank you for teaching me how to have a healthy, honest, and authentic relationship and for showing me what true intimacy is.

My mom and dad who are now in spirit, I love you so. Thank you for the life you brought me into. Thank you for letting me be myself, and thank you for always being there. I can hardly wait to see you again and to see what our next lives will be like together.

And my sisters—the Rubinetti girls—four of them (including me). I am so grateful for you all. Cre, you took care of me—and my kids—all of your life. I miss you so. Everyone should be so lucky as to have a big sister like you. I feel you with me all the time. Your love for me transcends any physical death, and so does mine for you. See you in my dreams. Donna, you have always made things better for me, easier for me, and more beautiful. You always willingly share all that you have with me and have become the keeper of Daddy's dry wit and humor. I am so glad you are my sister. Suzanne, all of my childhood memories are filled with you. You are in every frame of my mind, and you are in every experience I had more so than anyone else. Not only are you my sister but a powerful woman I admire. Thank you for the gift of your beautiful children: Alyssa, my goddaughter; Jessica; and Jimmy. They are treasures to our family. I love you all so very much.

And Michelle, my first niece, my littlest sister. Oh what fun Suzanne and I had with you when you were a baby. You were like our very own living doll. I remember the day you were born as if you were my own baby. Now a woman in your own right, taking the place of our fourth sister, the place held by your mother, I honor you and adore you. Thank you, Jody, for loving her and for giving us Kaylee—my goddaughter—and Jake.

My dear brothers George, Steve, and Jimmy—you may have come into my life through my sisters, but you are and always will be the family of my heart and soul. It brings me great joy to know how lucky my sisters are to be loved by you. Dor and Donna, thanks for always standing by me like bookends that hold me up and cheer me on. In lots of ways we are closer than sisters.

With love and thanks to all of the families that have welcomed me into their lives and hearts—Grandma Jane and Gramps; my friend and sister Karen; Tom and Joe; my wonderful, talented, smart, and sassy nephews Tommy, Joey, and Sean; and my goddaughter Carley. Thank you for making me, Jussie, and Nick your family. It has been great.

And to the Sebastianos, thank you for staying in my life and giving me the space for more. Joey, I will always be so grateful that you gave me Nick and Juss. Thank you.

My colleagues and fellow mediums and healers: thank you for a community that often resembles Hogwarts. Gary, Rita, Bobbie, Peg, Jenn, Gale, Anna A., Barbara A., Sal, Sheila, the Amato sisters, Evelyn, Diana, Jack, and Virginia—I am amazed and humbled by your gifts and wisdom. I am most honored to walk among you.

To my forever-in-this-lifetime-and-every-other friends Kim, Claire, and Maureen; two Lus, Vivian, Donna, Maria, Gina, Kim C., and for all my friends who have been my friends since childhood, high school, and my early twenties, I'm so glad we never parted. There are too many to name, but you know who you are. Can't wait to see what we look like in our nineties!

And my teachers—first and foremost, Eamonn. I am a product of your great teaching and mentoring. Jinny, you started this whole ball rolling. Brian and Simon, this book was conceived in your workshop in 2010, so technically you are the fathers. My highest gratitude to you all. Thank you for showing up.

And lastly, for all my yoga students and my clients—thank you for giving me a purpose. Thank you for teaching me so, so much. You inspire me and show me how it's done. Thank you for growing and expanding and making this world a better place. I feel safe knowing we walk this earth together. Your light shines bright, and I am so glad to know you all.

Discover more at:
www.rosemarierubinetticappiello.com

Email RoseMarie directly at:
ro@rosemarierubinetticappiello.com

About the Author
Rosemarie Rubinetti Cappiello

*Intuitive, medium, healer, hospice grief counselor and volunteer,
ordained spiritual minister, certified hypnotherapist, yoga instructor,
Reiki-attuned, BS in physical education from Montclair State University*

Trained by the best teachers from Arthur Findlay College in England, RoseMarie is a gifted medium, intuitive, and healer who has worked professionally in this capacity since 2000. Through thousands of private medium readings and platform medium demonstrations throughout New Jersey, New York, and Connecticut, she has connected many people to their loved ones in spirit. She feels completely privileged and blessed to do this work. Many people claim their lives change dramatically after having a reading with her, with the weight of grief and sadness significantly decreasing.

RoseMarie lives in New Jersey with her husband, John; children; and two dogs, Marco and Ruby. She is an adjunct at a local university, teaching yoga in the physical education department.

CPSIA information can be obtained at www.ICGtesting.com
Printed in the USA
BVOW04s2323100816

458317BV00009B/1/P